"Don't you realize that this is only a dream?" Erin said painfully.

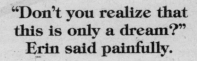

She tore her gaze from him. "I feel so . . . ." She groped for the right word.

"Frightened?" Ty provided, placing his hand beneath her chin and forcing her to meet his gaze.

"Yes," she admitted. "Scared, frightened, afraid to reach out for something I need desperately. To me, this is like a dream come true, Ty," she confessed, the words tumbling out. "It's a stolen moment in both our lives, something unexpected that came up out of nowhere. You take my breath away every time I think of you," she whispered.

"Erin," he commanded gently, "why do you see this time together as stolen moments? That once you leave, it's over."

A myriad of emotions clashed violently within her as she stared up into his clear blue eyes . . .

Dear Reader:

June 1983 marked SECOND CHANCE AT LOVE's second birthday—and we have good reason to celebrate! While romantic fiction has continued to grow, SECOND CHANCE AT LOVE has remained in the forefront as an innovative, top-selling romance series. In ever-increasing numbers you, the readers, continue to buy SECOND CHANCE AT LOVE, which you've come to know as the "butterfly books."

During the past two years we've received thousands of letters expressing your enthusiasm for SECOND CHANCE AT LOVE. In particular, many of you have asked: "What happens to the hero and heroine after they get married?"

As we attempted to answer that question, our thoughts led naturally to an exciting new concept—a line of romances based on married love. We're now proud to announce the creation of this new line, coming to you this fall, called TO HAVE AND TO HOLD.

There has never been a series of romances about marriage. As we did with SECOND CHANCE AT LOVE, we're breaking new ground, setting a new precedent. TO HAVE AND TO HOLD romances will be heartwarming, compelling love stories of marriages that remain exciting, adventurous, enriching and, above all, romantic. Each TO HAVE AND TO HOLD romance will bring you two people who love each other deeply. You'll see them struggle with challenges many married couples face. But no matter what happens, their love and commitment will see them through to a brighter future.

We're very enthusiastic about TO HAVE AND TO HOLD, and we hope you will be too. Watch for its arrival this fall. We will, of course, continue to publish six SECOND CHANCE AT LOVE romances every month in addition to our new series. We hope you'll read and enjoy them all!

Warm wishes,

Ellen Edwards

Ellen Edwards
SECOND CHANCE AT LOVE
The Berkley Publishing Group
200 Madison Avenue
New York, N.Y. 10016

ON WINGS OF PASSION
BETH BROOKES

A
SECOND CHANCE AT LOVE
BOOK

1

"BRUCE, I DON'T want this assignment," Erin pleaded with her boss. Her husky voice softened. "Please, you know how much I hate the Air Force. I can't be objective about this subject. Don't you understand?"

Unable to remain still a moment longer, she moved away from the desk and paced the room nervously. Bruce Lansbury watched her with a familiar inscrutable gaze she had come to dislike. It meant that he would have his way in the end. She clenched her hands into fists.

"Look, I've worked for *Newsday Magazine* for seven years and I've *never* turned down a major assignment, especially on a controversial issue. But I can't stand the Air Force, Bruce. I wouldn't give the investigation the fair treatment it's due."

"Erin, Erin," he soothed, putting down his pipe and rising from his chair to his lanky six-foot height. "I know you lost your husband in an Air Force accident. You've got good reason to hold a grudge. But I need your solid investigative abilities on this one."

Erin pushed a thick strand of dark hair off her shoulder. Usually she could maintain a professional demeanor, betraying no emotion. But this situation was different. It nudged the still-glowing coals of an old festering wound deep within her heart. She narrowed her blue eyes as she studied her boss.

His hands hanging loosely at his sides, he reminded her of a gawky eighteen-year-old basketball player who was all arms and legs. After she had graduated from college, Bruce had given her this job on one of the most widely read weekly magazines in the country. Since then, she had honed her skills until she'd become a top-notch investigator.

Now she compressed her full lips, studying him carefully. "You can't do this," she said. "Why do you want to assign me this story when you know my personal feelings about the Air Force?"

He shrugged and swept a hand through his salt-and-pepper hair. "Truthfully, Erin, we want an article that is stacked against the Air Force Triad recommendation that we purchase more bombers. The publisher feels we ought to concentrate our defense spending on land- and submarine-based missiles, that we should phase out the Strategic Air Command bombers, which form the third leg of the Triad concept. The public would be saved the enormous expense of purchasing one hundred B-1 bombers to replace the older B-52's. I want you to find facts to justify our stand." He scratched his head thoughtfully. "Go in there and prove we don't need the bomber wing." He gave her a slight smile. "Who knows? We might end up saving American taxpayers billions of dollars."

Erin gave up. "Then it's final? There's no way I can gracefully get out of this?"

"Jack assigned it to you at our editorial staff meeting this morning. I tried to discourage him because of your feelings about the Air Force." Bruce sighed and gave her an apologetic look. "I'm sorry. The job's all yours."

He opened the top drawer on the right-hand side of

his desk and pulled out a folder, which he handed to her. "You're booked on a flight tonight for Wright-Patterson Air Force Base, which is located near Dayton, Ohio. Captain Tynan Phillips, from the 410th Bomb Wing, has been assigned through the Pentagon to be your host. He'll meet you there."

Erin let out a shaky breath. "I don't believe this, Bruce."

"Erin, I tried to dissuade them." He squeezed her arm gently. "I'm sorry. I can see the pain in your eyes, but the job has to be done. In fact, you've got a real obstacle course to run before you fly in the B-52."

Her head snapped up, her eyes widening. "What are you talking about?"

Bruce returned to his desk and sat down, folding his frame like an accordion back into the leather chair. "The Strategic Air Command has decided they'd like the publicity we could provide, so they're giving you the red carpet treatment. It includes taking a ride on the mighty bomber itself."

Erin tried to control her dismay. "You've got to be kidding!"

"It's all part of SAC's treatment of special people," he assured her.

"Even hostile reporters?" She shot him a fiery glance.

"When I talked to Colonel Cox over at the Pentagon, he seemed to think SAC's honesty and credibility would change the mind of even the most ardent antimilitary reporter."

She clenched her fist. "Well, they're wrong this time."

Bruce cocked his head. "So you'll take the assignment?"

"Not willingly."

"Look, Erin, I've said I'm sorry and I am. But the

Air Force can't bring back your husband. When you stop to think that we've got a weekly circulation of six million, you realize how much influence this article could have, how many opinions you could change."

Erin rubbed her forehead, where an ache was beginning to throb. "That's a lot of people," she agreed softly. "My husband was killed a long time ago. I guess I should be over it by now." She lifted her chin and stared out the window at the New York skyline against the blue September day. "I just don't want to be reminded yet again, that's all."

"Nobody ever said living was easy," Bruce sympathized. "Starting tonight, you'll be in Dayton for two days. A month from now, you'll go to a place called Gwinn, Michigan."

Erin picked up her purse and adjusted it on her shoulder. "Where's that?"

"Someplace up near the Canadian border. That's where K. I. Sawyer, an SAC Air Force Base, is located. You'll have four more days worth of investigation there before hopping a flight on a B-52."

Erin shook her head. "You look like an excited kid, Bruce."

He grinned. "Can't help it. As much as I'm against the B-1 bomber, I wouldn't mind taking a ride on one of those B-52's."

"Then *you* take the assignment, and I'll play senior editor for the next week!"

He laughed. "I wish! Really, I do envy you a bit. I've always loved airplanes, especially the big ones."

Erin grimaced and headed for the door. "With my luck, I'll get caught on board when World War Three starts."

Bruce smiled, relighting his pipe and sucking noisily

on it. "Naw, that won't happen. Just do me a favor and don't rip that poor captain's head off. I understand he's a B-52 bomber pilot from Sawyer."

Erin stood in the doorway. "If he's smart, he'll stay out of my way."

"Well," Bruce murmured, puffing forcefully on the pipe, "I hope he's been trained to deal with strong-willed, temperamental Irishwomen, because he'll need it for you." He pointed at the folder under her arm. "Did you see his first name? Tynan. Bet that's Gaelic. I wonder if he's one of your countrymen."

Erin rolled her eyes. "Oh, Lord, that's all I need— an Irishman for a watchdog. Thanks, Bruce. Thanks a lot. Now I know you really want me to quit."

"Nope. Just remember—this is a choice assignment and management wouldn't send just anyone. You're the best, Erin, and they're counting on your abilities to find the evidence that'll stack the deck against the bombers and in favor of the missiles."

"Don't worry, I won't fail them on that point. Maybe you're right, Bruce. Maybe a little revenge will be healthy for my soul. I'll be in touch."

"Fine. Hey, just on the qt, if you do your usual good job, this assignment could probably earn you a nice raise and promotion."

Her eyebrows rose. That would be a plum. After roving from one end of the country to the other to research hard-hitting stories, she was getting tired of traveling. Bruce had told her that the associate editor's job would be available in a few months.

She winked at him. "Okay, you've convinced me. Just keep New York alive and well for me while I'm gone."

"I promise. Enjoy Dayton."

Erin closed the door softly behind her. It was almost four o'clock and her flight left at eight. She'd better hurry home and get ready.

The initial shock of having to fly out at a moment's notice wore off as Erin packed. She felt comfortable in designer jeans and a warm bulky pink sweater.

On her dresser was a photograph of her husband, Steve, in an Army officer's uniform. She paused to study the picture. It had been nine years since his death. She closed her eyes as painful memories filled her. Then the thought that he had been killed while flying an Air Force cargo plane renewed her anger. She held the picture against her chest, taking deep breaths to control her emotions.

She had married him straight out of high school. In recent years, she had realized she should have turned down Steve's proposal. They had grown up together in the same community. She had been a gawky freckle-faced high school freshman, and he'd been a senior ready to graduate. They had fallen in love, but Steve had had the wisdom to wait. If it was really right, waiting wouldn't change anything, he'd told her. He'd promised to come back for her after college, and he had.

It had come as no particular surprise when Steve joined ROTC in college and went on to become a regular Army officer. The sight of him in uniform when he'd arrived home to claim her for his own had melted her heart. At eighteen, she'd been like a young willow, unworldly and sensitive to the demands of being a military wife.

Erin placed the picture back on the dresser and, pushing her memories to a dark compartment of her heart, concentrated on packing.

* * *

That night she blinked against the strong light of the Dayton Airport terminal as she emerged from the plane. She had piled her hair on top of her head and changed into a tailored suit of dusty beige and a burnt-sienna blouse of raw silk. She felt mentally prepared to meet the Air Force officer who was to be her escort.

At ten at night the airport wasn't very busy and Erin halted, searching the small crowd anxiously waiting for friends and relatives. A slow anger began to burn as she quickly scanned their faces for an Air Force officer. Just like the military to let her down, she fumed, gripping her leather briefcase tightly.

As she headed down a long corridor toward the baggage area, she sensed rather than saw someone at her side. Before she heard his low, carefully modulated voice, she felt his presence.

"Miss Quinlan?"

She drew in a deep breath and spun around. Her lips parted as she met and held his gaze. His eyes were a warm, inviting blue, and she sensed his care and concern as he stood looking down at her. His eyes sparkled with a hawklike intensity that sent a shiver through her. His hair was black, and she could see signs of his Irish heritage in the narrow planes of his high-cheekboned face. Despite the creases at the corners of his eyes and mouth, there was a certain youthfulness about him. She guessed he was in his mid-thirties.

Erin couldn't tear her gaze from his intelligent expression. As much as she wanted to dislike him, she couldn't. Her eyes were drawn to his mouth. It was well chiseled and strong and the corners turned up in an appealing manner. Just looking at him, she could tell he had a sense of humor, and for some reason that thought made her feel less threatened by his nearness. He stood straight, his shoulders broad, his stance relaxed. His smile widened as he removed his hat and inclined his head toward her.

"Since I'm an expert at detecting the Irish, you must be Erin Quinlan."

Something in his tone—or perhaps it had to do with the tingle his deep voice sent down her spine—aroused Erin's anger. Her nostrils flared and she stepped back from him. His masculinity overwhelmed her. "I'm Erin Quinlan," she said, her voice low with fury. "And don't try to pretend to know me just because we're both Irish." She placed a hand on her hip and watched for his reaction. She wouldn't let him sweet-talk her into writing anything but the truth about his lousy Air Force.

His eyes darkened and he studied her with new interest, surprise registering on his clean-cut features. Replacing the hat, he said, "I'm Captain Ty Phillips."

"Obviously," she drawled, turning abruptly and heading down the hall. Her behavior surprised her. She was acting—and feeling—like a mesmerized eighteen-year-old. Ty Phillips was incredibly male in every sense of the word, and her head was spinning from their brief encounter. More than anything, she wanted to get as far away from him as possible.

As she tried to shake off his effect, she became aware that he was walking at her side, easily keeping pace. "Do you always greet strangers with such kind words?" he asked with just a hint of sarcasm. He glanced at her out of the corner of his eye.

Erin pressed her lips together to stifle her retort. She could see he wasn't going to take anything sitting down. Well, that figured. She couldn't expect someone from the Air Force to be diplomatic! "As far as I'm concerned, Captain," she said through gritted teeth, "anyone from the Air Force doesn't deserve better treatment." She halted, turning around and glaring up at him. "If you expected some sweet little lady from the big city who would giggle like a schoolgirl, you were very much mistaken."

Ty Phillips raised his eyebrows and regarded her closely. "I hadn't expected you to be so openly hostile, Miss Quinlan. Where I come from, a little courtesy goes a long way. I certainly wouldn't treat anyone with the rudeness you've just exhibited."

Erin's lips parted as she stared back at him. "Why—"

He gripped her arm, turning her around and forcing her to start walking. "They told me you were an antimilitary reporter," he went on. "That I can live with, Miss Quinlan. But I won't put up with a shrew who pretends to be a reporter." She shot him a scathing look, but he continued, unperturbed. "Now that we've made proper introductions and know where we stand with one another, let's pick up your baggage."

Erin jerked her arm away. "I thought all you public affairs officers were supposed to be smiling two-faced liars."

Ty Phillips grinned self-confidently. "First, I'm not a public affairs officer. Second, I was assigned this job, Miss Quinlan, in addition to my normal flight duties at Sawyer Air Force Base. Third, I don't like people who form ideas about other people before they've completed a proper investigation. And last, I'm not all sweetness and light. Public affairs officers have diplomacy. I don't."

Erin marched ahead, her jaw set. "That's obvious!" she retorted.

"Why don't you make this easy on both of us and just be civil?"

She halted, anger making her voice tremble. "Captain,

I was forced to take this assignment, just like you were! I don't want to be here. I don't want to have to spend one extra minute around you. I don't want *anything* to do with your damned Air Force!"

He stood tensely, hands on hips, eyes darkening thunderclouds. "Someone ought to take you over his knee and give you a good spanking."

Erin smirked and stepped onto the escalator. "Wishful thinking, Captain. I suppose in my investigation of the Air Force I'll find you're all wife beaters, too."

"I'm sure you'd like to think that," he answered, his voice barely above a growl. "You probably have your husband completely cowed."

Erin marched off the escalator and immediately spotted her luggage on the baggage turntable. "I'm widowed, Captain, so it's a moot point, isn't it?"

Ty Phillips walked easily at her side. "I suppose it is, but a good-looking woman like you had better watch her step."

She grimaced at him. "I learned one thing about Irishmen a long time ago, Captain. They're so full of bluff that it's laughable. You have the wonderful job of escorting me around for the next two days. You don't like it and neither do I. You're such a typical male chauvinist it makes me ill. Go talk to some other woman who will believe your blarney."

Her heart pounded violently as she saw and felt his reaction. He reached out, his fingers sinking into the soft flesh of her upper arm, and pulled her to a stop. He was so close she felt his hot breath against her cheek. His once-kind eyes had turned bluer and predatorlike as he glared down at her. "Now, look," he rasped softly, "you may be a grown woman, but if you continue to act like a spoiled brat, I'll take you in hand, darlin'! You either begin acting civilly, or I'll put you over my knee right here in the middle of this airport."

A host of reactions exploded within her. She was aware of his male scent and the subtle excitement it produced in her. She recoiled at the talon-edged sharpness of his threat. Her lips parted and she stood very still within his grip. She knew he would do exactly as he promised. Swallowing hard, she tried to pull away from him but his fingers tightened, sending a painful warning up her arm.

"You're hurting me!" she whispered.

"You've hurt me too," he retorted, his fingers relaxing slightly against her flesh. "You can hate me and the Air Force, Miss Quinlan, but do me one favor. Treat the people we've got to deal with in the next few days without the rudeness you've displayed here. That's not too much to ask, is it? Or are you ice all the way through?"

Erin gasped. Heat rushed up her neck and into her face. "Why, you—!" she raged.

"Put a leash on that temper," he said softly, his eyes glittering dangerously.

She stood frozen. Seconds crystallized into what seemed like hours of agony because of his nearness. Eventually she was aware of his fingers loosening their grip on her arm. He straightened up, allowing his hand to fall to his side.

"Would you like to start all over?" he asked quietly.

She was trembling and close to exploding. She wanted to lash out and strike his suddenly expressionless face. It was as if all his previous warmth and friendliness had now been hidden deep within him. She was seeing another side of him, and it shook her deeply. He looked like someone who could easily send a nuclear warhead down the throat of his enemy. And right then he was looking at her as if she were the target.

Something old and painful broke loose within her heart and anguish surged to the surface. She fought it as her eyes filled with hot tears. She wouldn't cry! Not now. And not in front of this damned officer! Turning, she dashed the tears away with the back of her hand and headed blindly for her baggage. She reached down to pick up her only suitcase, but Ty Phillips took it from her and swung it up and over the turnstile. He was frowning and his eyes seemed to lighten slightly as he regarded her. Slowly, his expression softened. Erin reminded herself that he possessed a temper like her own—only he seemed much more in control of his than she was of hers.

"Come on, I have a car parked out front," he said, his voice clipped.

Erin followed him without comment. At the moment all she wanted was to get to the hotel and away from him. He led her to a dark-blue Air Force car parked along the curb. She reached out to open the door.

"I'll do that," he muttered, his fingers closing on the handle where her own fingers rested. She jerked her hand back as if it was burned. He gave her a disgruntled look and pulled the door open without another word. She slid into the seat, her hands resting tensely in her lap as he stowed the luggage in the trunk. She tensed as he slid behind the wheel and shut the car door.

Darkness swallowed them up as he drove away from the airport. Erin was thankful for the shadows. They hid what she knew must be apparent on her face. Feeling completely disoriented, she tried to compose herself. No man had ever attacked her as fiercely as Ty Phillips had. But a voice whispered that she had never been as rude to anyone as she had been to Ty. Compressing her lips, she stared blindly out the window. The silence in the car grew palpable.

Exhaustion crept over her. Rubbing her aching head, Erin felt the remains of her anger subside. She glanced at Captain Phillips, strongly aware of his presence. Even as he drove, an aura of quiet strength and control emanated from him, a determined steadiness that attracted her like a magnet.

"I don't know if anyone has briefed you on the itinerary," he said, interrupting her thoughts.

She raised her chin from her hand and looked at him across the seat. His voice was devoid of anger, and she relaxed a little. "No . . . I was given this assignment just this afternoon, so I'm flying blind."

"We certainly don't want you to do that."

"Poor choice of words," she admitted wearily. "No pun intended."

He turned, glancing at her briefly. She tensed again, feeling his careful appraisal, afraid he could see into her heart and mind. One moment he was attacking her, the next he displayed gentleness and warmth. She'd never known a man with such a quixotic personality.

She smiled grimly. She had to admit she was pretty volatile herself. Maybe it was the Irish in both of them.

"We're due over to the physiological medical facility at eight tomorrow morning," Captain Phillips informed her. "You'll be going through high altitude simulator training in order to qualify you to ride in our B-52."

"I'll just go through the motions," she mumbled.

"It will require your active participation," he corrected, his voice hardening. "You'd better take this training seriously, Miss Quinlan. Your life may depend on it."

"How?" she scoffed, meeting his gaze. Why did he keep contradicting her?

"I'm not going to give you a dissertation on it tonight," he said. "You'll be flying with us at between three hundred feet and thirty-nine thousand feet for ten hours. The cabin is pressurized for eight thousand feet. It's a military training mission and none of the comforts of commercial flying will be available—no stewardess, no magazines, no in-flight movies. If we get a decompression leak, you've got to be able to detect signs of hypoxia. Either that or you could become unconscious in a very short time." He glanced at her. "I for one don't want that to happen aboard my bomber. It would be one more black mark I'm sure you'd be quick to hold against me."

She ignored his jab. "What's hypoxia?"

"Oxygen starvation. The symptoms are subtle, which is one reason you'll be going through this test. Everybody gets different symptoms, and you have to be able to recognize your own."

"What are the chances of the bomber losing oxygen?"

"Not very great," he admitted, "but we're prepared to handle even remote possibilities. And since you'll be hitching a ride with us, you'll get some of that training."

"How sensible of the Air Force," she drawled sarcastically.

"Isn't it? We care about your neck, even if you don't."

She smiled tightly. "I'm touched, Captain. Still, your concern isn't going to earn you a gold star in my article."

"I don't believe in brownnosing, Miss Quinlan. When it comes to hostile reporters, the Air Force feels it can rely on its own integrity. What you write is your business.

Most reporters who are out to cut us down end up thinking differently after we've taken them through the training and briefings." He caught her skeptical gaze. "Most reporters are honest enough to be fair in their assessments of the Air Force. But there are always a few who are out to grind a personal ax regardless of the truth."

Erin narrowed her eyes. "Are you insinuating that I'd lie just to punish the Air Force?"

He shrugged. "I'll reserve comment until I see you under other circumstances."

She gritted her teeth. "I've never lied! Never! I have a reputation for being honest, and I'm not about to stoop to the Air Force's level of lies just to get a sensational story!"

Ty Phillips threw her a stony smile. "The Air Force doesn't lie. If it becomes a matter of security, then I'll inform you of such, Miss Quinlan. You'll be able to take your camera and shoot just about any pictures you want. I'll be around to try to answer all your questions. Contrary to what you seem to believe, we don't pull any punches."

Erin bit back a retort. In another two days she would be rid of him. Then it would be another month before she had to fly in the bomber that was slated to take off from K. I. Sawyer Air Force Base in Michigan. With that in mind, she allowed her anger to fade. *Two days,* she prayed silently. *Give me the patience and diplomacy to get through them without blowing this assignment.*

"I still don't see why it's necessary for me to ride on that ridiculous bomber in order to fulfill the requirements of my story," she said.

He glanced at her. "I understand you're taking the position that the Air Force should get rid of the Buff in the Triad concept."

She was confused. "What's the Buff?" she asked.

Captain Phillips grinned. "Sorry, that's Air Force lingo. We usually call the B-52 bomber the Buff. The men who fly it are referred to as Buff drivers."

Erin was surprised by the sudden warmth and pride in his voice. His expression relaxed, and she felt drawn to him. "Why is it called the Buff?" she asked.

"Ever seen a B-52?"

"A long time ago," she admitted hesitantly, bemused by the feeling of intimacy he had quickly established between them.

"They're a rather squat-looking bomber with a very long wingspan," he explained. "Not exactly the glamour girl of the big aircraft, or heavies, as they're called. Someone down the line coined a few choice words for the bomber. Buff stands for big ugly fat..." He grinned boyishly. "I'll leave the other *f* to your imagination."

She suppressed her own smile and, avoiding his eyes, stared out the window into the darkness. "And I suppose the Buff is such an unwieldy aircraft that you don't fly it, you drive it, right?" she asked, trying to sound casual. But in her mind's eye she kept seeing his warm eyes shining with enthusiasm.

His laughter was spontaneous and infectious, and it helped relieve the brittle tension between them. "You said it. You'll find out all about it when you fly that ten-hour mission with me and my crew."

She pursed her lips. If she didn't know better, she'd think he was looking forward to it, despite their initial antagonism. "I've never flown anywhere for that long," she said, surprised to realize it.

"There's a first time for everything, Miss Quinlan. And believe me, on this assignment I think you'll experience a lot of firsts."

"Is that a threat or a promise?" she asked, meeting his eyes.

He repressed a mischievous smile. "A promise. You know, not many civilians get the privilege of flying in a Buff. The Air Force doesn't honor many requests."

"I suppose droves of people are knocking down your doors to do just that," she said dryly.

He shrugged. "According to public affairs, it's a pretty common request. Despite what you think, many people consider the Buff an important deterrent."

Erin frowned and rubbed her forehead. She hated people who mouthed the words of their superiors without thinking for themselves. But for some reason Ty Phillips didn't strike her as anyone's puppet. "Is that you or the Air Force talking, Captain?" she asked.

His glance at her was sharp. "Let's get another thing straight," he said firmly. "I'm a Buff pilot, not a public affairs officer with a degree in media manipulation. Whenever you ask me a question, you'll get *my* answer, not the official Air Force response. Understand?"

"My goodness, what would your commanding officer say?" she teased.

"If Colonel McCaffery was worried about my mouth or my opinions, he would have assigned someone else."

"Then it's obvious you're considered politically safe, someone who will always back the Air Force's philosophy a hundred and ten percent."

A slow grin came to his mobile mouth. She was beginning to feel outmaneuvered. He hadn't fallen for her bait.

"Let's put it another way, Miss Quinlan," he told her. "Word came down through the squadron that they were asking for volunteers to escort you around. When it became known that you were a reporter, there were no takers. The major who heads up Public Affairs at Sawyer is out for an operation, and the young lieutenant temporarily in charge has been up to his ears in work, so he couldn't do it." He met her widened stare. "I was ordered to accept the job of escorting you."

"I hope you survive," she said dryly.

Ty smiled grimly and returned his attention to driving. "Darlin', if I can make it through survival training, I can survive you. The real question is, can you survive *me?*"

Erin folded her arms across her chest without replying. She'd been able to handle ninety percent of the people she had ever interviewed with ease. But Ty Phillips made her feel at a distinct disadvantage. She had always had the idea that a bomber pilot was slow-witted, at the bottom of his graduating class. But that certainly wasn't true of him. Disgruntled, she settled back in the seat, hoping to end the conversation. For a few minutes neither of them spoke.

Finally Ty asked her, "Have you had much background on the SAC mission and Triad?"

She roused herself from a half sleep. "No . . . I'm supposed to be getting some information on it from the Pentagon when I get back to New York."

"Does your publisher think he'll save the country a lot of money by getting rid of the Buffs?"

"I suppose," she murmured, too tired to comment.

"You don't sound sure."

"I sound tired," she replied irritably.

"Sorry."

Immediately she felt contrite and turned to look at him. Streetlights played over his face, creating glimmers and shadows. Her heart wrenched with newly awakening feelings. Suddenly she realized that he was just as exhausted as she was, yet he was trying to be courteous by keeping the conversation flowing. She was amazed at the emotions that registered on his face and in the depths of his dark eyes. She lifted her hand in a placating gesture. "No, I'm the one who should be sorry," she apologized. "It's just been a long, incredibly stressful day."

He gave her an enigmatic smile and turned the car into a hotel parking lot. "You're worth putting up with," was all he said. She gave him a skeptical look, unsure how to interpret his comment. He parked and turned off the engine. "Come on, there are reservations for us here. A hot bath and a good night's sleep ought to put you in a better frame of mind for tomorrow."

Erin felt emotionally and physically drained. Suddenly all her residual anger at him evaporated. Was it because he had met her barbs tactfully but firmly? Or, a voice whispered, was it because he was friendly and able to set her at ease with just a few words? Groaning silently, she refused to consider the answers too closely.

She was pleasantly surprised when he opened the car door for her. He extended his hand and wrapped his fingers firmly around her elbow. A small shiver coursed up her arm. She was keenly aware of his masculine appeal. Giving her a brief, almost official smile, he escorted her through the lobby of the hotel.

Blinking against the strong lights, and too tired to think, she let him handle the details at the registration desk. He had an aura of authority, and as she let him take charge, she realized in the back of her fuzzy mind that it meant she trusted him. The thought irritated her.

In no time at all, he had escorted her to her room. After placing her small suitcase at the foot of the bed, he handed her the keys.

He studied her in the semidarkness. "I know you civilians usually sleep in late, but how about if I come about six-thirty tomorrow morning? We'll have breakfast here before going to the Physiology Center."

She ignored her racing pulse and murmured with a vague wave, "Sounds fine. Good night." She thought she caught a mischievous glimmer in his eyes as he nodded and turned away, leaving the room. She stood staring after him, hands on hips. Was he laughing at her?

She frowned thoughtfully, then dismissed the matter. Right now, all she wanted was a hot bath and sleep.

2

"WHY WERE YOU silently laughing at me last night?"
Erin asked, not expecting an honest answer. She sat
opposite Ty Phillips at a booth in the hotel coffee shop
very early the next morning, idly stirring her coffee. He
looked incredibly handsome in his dark-blue uniform
with the silver captain's bars on his broad shoulders. His
dark hair still glistened from a shower, and she was aware
of his clean male scent. The shadows she had seen beneath his eyes the night before were gone and he looked
relaxed and refreshed, brimming with energy. He glanced
up at her, his long fingers cradling his own coffee cup.

"I wasn't laughing at you," he said. "Matter of fact,
I felt rather guilty for baiting you about civilians sleeping
in late. You didn't even respond to my teasing, so I knew
you really were exhausted." He grinned good-naturedly.
"I honestly expected you to snap something in return."

She sipped her coffee. "You felt guilty about ribbing
a civilian?" she scoffed.

He shrugged. "I have to remind myself that, even
though you can give as good as you get, I shouldn't take
advantage of the situation."

Erin lifted her chin, mildly irritated. "I don't like to
fight, Captain Phillips. It's not in my nature to go around
with a drawn sword."

"You could have fooled me." He chuckled. "We certainly managed to get off on the wrong foot yesterday." He watched her closely for a reaction.

She frowned. "I suppose in your estimation I'm a first-class pain."

"Do you care what I think?"

Her heart skipped a beat. She wanted to say no, but his warm eyes compelled her to be honest. "Yes," she muttered, shifting uncomfortably in the seat.

"I think you're a first-class Irish banshee," he said in a teasing tone. "And I think your reaction to me at the airport had something to do with your past and not with me personally."

Erin swallowed hard, unable to meet his probing gaze. How in the world had an Air Force officer become *that* intuitive? His comment had shaken her to the core, and she stared down at her coffee cup with unseeing eyes. "You have a blunt way of speaking about very personal matters," she said evenly.

"I think it's called perception," he said gently. "Don't worry, Erin, I won't ever use that knowledge against you."

Her heart twisted, and she forced herself to meet his warming gaze. Her lips parted at the tenderness in his expression. He meant it. He would never deliberately hurt her.

Emotions clashed within her. How could she trust any Air Force officer? Hadn't the Air Force killed her husband? But as hard as she tried to resurrect her old anger, it simply refused to be prodded back to life. He had guessed that there were reasons she had behaved so rudely and had already forgiven her. Suddenly she felt afraid.

"Look," she muttered, "why don't you fill me in on

the essential details of our trip to Wright-Patterson?" She drew out a legal pad and pen from her purse.

If he was upset by her sudden brusqueness, he didn't show it. "Let's order breakfast first," he suggested. "I don't operate well on an empty stomach."

She glanced at him sharply, suppressing the urge to snap. He had done nothing to deserve a blistering retort from her. "Fine," she agreed.

Over a large breakfast of three eggs, hash browns, and toast, Ty said in a friendly manner, "You know, you might end up liking K. I. Sawyer. It's a Northern Tier base near the Canadian border." He raised an eyebrow, stealing a quick look at her. "If you like the wilderness and hiking in the autumn, you'll enjoy your stay with us."

"I'm surprised you haven't already decided what I do and don't like, Captain."

He quelled a smile, concentrating on his meal. "Let's just say I've made some guesses," he drawled.

Erin hated herself for getting trapped by his easy-going manner, but she couldn't resist asking, "Such as?"

"Such as, you're tall and athletically built. Since you're from a city, that probably means you play tennis or jog. You don't strike me as a gal who sits behind a desk for long before becoming restless."

"So far so good," she admitted, frowning.

"Want me to go on?"

"Sure, I always like to see someone with foot-in-mouth disease."

"Remember, you asked me to volunteer my first impressions." He laid his fork on the table and leaned back, studying her carefully, a soft smile curving his mouth. "You have a terrible temper—that's already been well established." He flashed a boyish grin. "Of course, your being Irish automatically atones for that particular weakness."

"Weakness!"

He raised a hand. "I'm not finished. Now, sit there like the beautiful lady you are and let's see how close I come. You're a woman of great sensitivity. It would be easy for anyone to affect you either negatively or positively. I think you need quiet time to pull yourself together. I don't see you as someone who can stand a lot of stress without retreating to your favorite place and healing yourself. So," he continued, his expression suddenly very serious, "you hide your vulnerability beneath a tough exterior, playing the role of a no-nonsense, hard-hitting reporter who can take it on the nose."

Erin clutched her napkin tightly in her lap. He had no business commenting on her like this! "Believe me," she said icily, "I can be as tough as the situation requires."

"Can't everyone?"

"Of course not."

His eyes held hers. "You don't need to thrust that tough image out in front of you, Erin," he said softly. "Why are you so afraid of allowing people to get close to you?"

She flushed under his intense scrutiny. "I don't know who you are—"

He leaned forward, his elbows on the table. "Just a Buff pilot, darlin'. So don't look at me like that."

"Like what?"

"Like you're going to explode. Come on, relax. I told you before, I'll never use my perceptions of you against you, Erin. But obviously you don't believe that."

She wrestled with her confusing emotions. "Let's talk about business, shall we?" she demanded coldly, anxious to change the topic.

"Anything you want. Where would you like to start?"

Erin's fingers trembled as they closed around her pen and she positioned the pad on the table. Who *was* this Captain Ty Phillips? She felt stripped beneath his scrutiny, and her throat constricted with a familiar paralyzing fear.

When had that fear begun to haunt her? Soon after her husband's death. Life had been so secure until then. Suddenly she had been thrown abruptly out into the mainstream of life, trying to recover from the emotional loss as well as survive in a hard, uncaring world. And now this officer had dropped into her life and was nonchalantly exposing her deeply hidden wounds and anxieties.

It required her concentrated effort to push aside her feelings and return to business. "Tell me about the Triad," she suggested.

He was very willing to describe it. "Very simply, it's a defense concept to keep this country free from aggression," he explained. "It consists of SAC B-52 bombers, intercontinental ballistic missiles—which you will probably want to refer to as ICBM's—and Navy submarine sea-launched missiles. The three forms of defense guarantee that, if an outside force penetrates one leg of our defense system, it must take on the other two. As a consequence, SAC plays a defensive role on a global front, and we keep aggressive powers somewhat in line."

"My editor feels you can do away with the land-based bombers," Erin challenged.

Ty shrugged. "That becomes a matter of opinion, Erin. Of the three forms I've mentioned, only the bombers can be recalled from a target. If there were a threat of nuclear war, would you rather push a button to launch an ICBM, or send bombers that you knew could come back in case the situation deescalated?"

She raised her chin, watching him. Gone was the boyish quality she'd seen before. Now he was strictly a military officer telling her what he obviously believed in. "I'd want the bombers," she admitted. "That's only logical."

"I think so, too. And so does the Air Force. Which is why we've put the B-1 B bomber in production to replace the Buff."

"But you're talking billions of dollars."

He sighed, pushing a fork absently around on the tabletop. "What's peace worth to you? The Buff is twenty-four years old and is rapidly becoming an obsolete way to defend our country. The Buff is so old that the Air Force, rather than private companies, has to manufacture some of the parts for it. No one else in the aircraft industry still makes them. This affects the bomber's reliability in the long run. The first fifteen B-1 B's will be completed in a few years. We're in a pretty precarious position right now without them."

Erin was perplexed. "So far you're telling me how much money we're spending to keep the Buffs flying. Surely they must be doing the job—"

He shook his head. "It's more complicated than that, Erin. The overall defense systems of unfriendly countries are becoming more capable all the time. They have surface-to-air missiles, or SAM's, and newer radar techniques. The Buff is too large to evade radar and it's got too little room for us to add the necessary electronics needed to get it safely through to its assigned targets."

"Will the B-1 overcome these problems?"

He nodded. "On all counts," he promised grimly.

Erin scribbled down a few more notes.

"If"—he took a deep breath and shook his head—"and I hope it never comes to that, but if there were a limited nuclear war, the Buff would not be a solid deterrent. In other words, one third of our Triad concept is weakened by the problems I just mentioned. And if we know that, you can bet our enemies do too."

"This is positively gruesome. I hate the thought of war," she admitted, searching his face.

"That makes two of us, darlin'. You'll find that the SAC bomber crews are more concerned about peace than most people think. We don't want to fight a war. We'd much rather act as a deterrent and keep the peace."

Erin heard the slight tremble in his voice, and it affected her deeply. "I always thought you guys were real hawks, waiting for a war to begin."

He shook his head. "I won't try to persuade you one way or the other. Instead, I think spending a few days around us will give you a chance to form your own opinions."

"But I'm a captive audience. I'm willing to listen."

"No way, darlin'. We'll let the facts speak for themselves. Fair enough?"

She nodded, impressed with his fairness. If he had tried to influence her, she would have resented him, and probably rejected his opinions. As it was, he had made her more curious and perhaps more receptive to his news. She closed her pad and put the pen away. "So where to now?" she asked.

Ty settled the blue flight cap on his head and stood up. "We'll get you qualified to ride in a Buff. You need a card from the medical center saying that you've taken the course and lived to tell about it." He flashed her a reassuring smile and held out his hand.

She hesitated only briefly. His fingers were warm and surprisingly firm as he helped her from the booth, and he seemed to release her hand with reluctance.

The Physiology Center, a single-story barracks set on a grassy knoll, was located just inside the entrance gates of Wright-Patterson Air Force Base. As Ty ushered Erin inside, a booming voice carried down the hall.

"Damned if it isn't an SAC trained killer. Phillips! How the hell are you?"

Erin glanced at Ty to see his reaction to the name calling; he looked slightly embarrassed. An officer in his mid-fifties came striding forward, hand extended, a wide smile on his narrow face.

"Colonel, good to see you again," Ty murmured.

The lieutenant colonel gripped Ty's hand and shook it heartily. "I couldn't believe it when they called and said you were coming. Good Lord, how many years has it been since I flew with you?"

Erin stood back, enjoying the warm exchange. The colonel was a man of slight, wiry build and his peppered mustache made him look almost like a civilian instead of a military officer.

Ty introduced her. "This is Erin Quinlan from *Newsday Magazine*. Erin, this is Colonel John McIntire, the head of this chamber of horrors."

"Ah, don't listen to this guy," he told Erin, smiling and gripping her hand. "Nice to meet you, Ms. Quinlan. We're privileged to have you come down and see what goes on in training these Buff drivers and tanker toads."

A smile tugged at Erin's lips, and she cast a glance at Ty. "Tanker toads?" she echoed, trying not to laugh.

Ty grinned. "Stick around for more than a day and we'll have you talking like an SAC professional," he promised.

"Tanker toads is an affectionate term we use for the crews who refuel the Buffs while they're in flight," McIntire explained.

"And SAC trained killers?" she asked wryly. "It has an ominous ring, Colonel."

McIntire slapped Ty on the back. "Naw, just another term used with respect for the fine job these guys do. During my orientation on the different aircraft flown in the Air Force, I had the privilege of being on Ty's crew. He was just a young co then, still wet behind the ears."

"Co is another word for copilot," Ty explained. "You'll find we abbreviate everything or make it into a set of initials." He turned to McIntire. "We about ready to get this show on the road?"

"You bet. First let me show Ms. Quinlan around."

"Call me Erin," she invited, surprised at her friendliness. She frowned inwardly, displeased with how easily their affability won her over.

"Lovely name for a lovely woman. You're a lucky fella, Phillips."

Ty winked at Erin. "Jealousy will get you nowhere, Colonel McIntire. Let's show her your steel box."

Erin followed both officers to the center of the room, where a large rectangular metal chamber dominated.

"This is our hyperbaric chamber, Erin," McIntire explained. "We train people who have to fly at high altitudes how to survive in case of rapid or slow decompression. We also teach them about hypoxia and symptoms of oxygen deprivation so they'll live to tell about it. Later in the day you'll be going in there for about two hours."

Erin walked cautiously inside the imposing white chamber. It was constructed from thick metal panels riveted together by huge bolts. Since the chamber could be made to simulate any altitude, it had to be strong enough to withstand the pressure created by the atmosphere inside. Several chairs were attached to the chamber's outside walls near small, very thick panels of glass. Inside were two rows of benches, each with individual instrument panels and assorted oxygen hoses draped nearby. Erin repressed a shiver. Maybe Ty was right. Maybe it was a chamber of horrors. But the way McIntire talked, it seemed nothing to be alarmed about. Uneasy, she followed them out of the chamber to a classroom.

There she sat for three hours learning about the effects of high altitude on an unprotected body. Ty had disappeared at the beginning. Growing bored, she idly jotted down a few notes. Although the airmen giving the various lectures were good, clear speakers, she couldn't keep her mind on what they were saying. Words such as *hypoxia*, *decompression*, and *the bends* were mentioned repeatedly.

Her thoughts kept wandering back to Ty. She rested her chin in her palm and stared down at the doodles on her pad. Why did she already feel such an accepted part of this crazy military family? She had noticed that the officers treated the enlisted men and women almost as equals yet she had always thought that there was a distinct division in the armed services between officers and enlisted people. She let out a long sigh, completely perplexed.

At lunch Ty reappeared, ambling over to her desk.

"Well, did you learn anything so far?" he asked.

She glanced up at him briefly. "You want the truth?"

"Always."

"I'm bored to death. I keep asking myself what good all this will do and what it has to do with riding in a Buff."

Ty cocked his head, a warning glitter in his blue eyes. "I know it's hard to understand, Erin, but if we get a rapid decompression, you could be dead in a matter of minutes. This boring information could literally save your life."

She felt properly chastised. "Okay, okay. I'll try to listen more attentively after lunch."

"We nearly lost a crew member about a year ago to this very thing," Ty went on, sitting down at the desk next to hers. He rubbed his face tiredly. "We were up at thirty-nine thousand feet and we got an RD—rapid decompression. Our gunner, Davis, was on his last mission with us before he was to be transferred. He was asleep on the bunk. The new gunner got his own mask on and then fought his way forward to clap the mask over Davis."

Erin frowned. "And?"

"You have to keep in mind that during RD we take emergency flight maneuvers. I nosed the Buff down and was dropping her like a rock to reach ten thousand feet. At that altitude you can survive. But for the gunner to move against the building g forces to get to Davis was damn near impossible. By the time the gunner reached him, Davis's heart had stopped beating."

Erin put her hand against her lips, her eyes widening. She searched Ty's face anxiously. "Oh . . . I didn't realize . . ."

He held her startled gaze. "No one ever does until it

happens," he muttered. He reached over and pulled her hand away from her mouth. "That's why I don't want anything to happen to you, gal. I came too damn close to losing a man, and there's no way I'm losing you. So be good and work hard this afternoon."

He released her hand and stood up. "Come on, I don't want to completely ruin your appetite. John McIntire is waiting to take us over to the officers' club for lunch."

Erin rose, troubled. "What happened to Davis? Did he live?"

"Barely. The other gunner had to administer cardio-pulmonary resuscitation. I landed the Buff at the closest available base. We had air traffic scrambled for a hundred miles in all directions. It was a life-and-death situation, and I wasn't going to go by the book to get him down and to a hospital. It caused a few hard feelings, until the tower learned what was happening." He grimaced, opening the door for her. "It was too close, Erin. Much too close."

On the way to the car, Erin considered his story. She was impressed by the difficult job he had, and by the decisiveness required to handle such an emergency situation. Once Ty's arm brushed hers as they walked side by side, and immediately their eyes met. His were warm and open, and something deep inside her, some hard core of pain and anger, seemed to melt. She looked away, confused.

John McIntire drove them to the officers' club and ushered them into the dining room, where they helped themselves to a buffet lunch. Erin took a seat across the table from McIntire. Ty sat down next to her.

"You ought to know you're being escorted by one of the finest Buff pilots in SAC, Erin," McIntire said, smiling amiably. "I knew him when he was a green kid just out of the Air Force Academy. He impressed me even then." He shook his head. "Funny how you can tell who will and won't make it in this pressure-cooker business."

Erin placed her napkin in her lap. "How is it a pressure cooker?" she asked.

"Tell her, Ty," McIntire urged.

Ty rested his chin against his folded hands and gazed thoughtfully at her. "It might bore you," he hedged.

"Nothing you've said so far has bored me, Captain Phillips."

A glint of humor danced in his eyes as he held her gaze. "Sure?"

"Very sure. Want me to swear to it?"

"That won't be necessary. What John is referring to is the fact that SAC bomber crews are under a lot of pressure from headquarters to do an incredible amount of testing. Each division is allotted so much fuel for the B-52's. If we've already flown our required number of hours for a particular month and still haven't burned up the fuel budgeted to us, we have to fly more missions until it's used up." He pursed his lips. "On an average I'd say we spend seventy hours a week on duty and twenty days out of the month away from home."

Erin stared at him in surprise. "Twenty days away from home every month? Good Lord, that's ridiculous." In her own brief time as a military wife she had never had to face such a strain. Steve had been stationed near a populated city and had stayed on the base most of the time. She'd been free to pursue her education.

"It's a terrible strain on the family and marital ties," he admitted.

McIntire nodded sadly. "Ty can attest to that from personal experience," he said softly.

Ty said nothing, but Erin saw a momentary flash of

pain in his eyes. She'd occasionally wondered about his
marital status and hadn't noticed a wedding ring, which
had surprised her. He seemed far too handsome and intelligent not to be married. But why did she suddenly
~~feel~~ glad that he was single? *Stop it,* she chided herself.
It doesn't mean a thing.

"You find out in a real hurry just what your marriage
is made of if you marry an SAC pilot," McIntire told
her in a confidential tone. "A lot of women can't adjust
to the demands that SAC puts on their men. Belonging
to the military means making constant compromises in
your personal life."

She shook her head. "You make it sound as if the
divorce rate is higher than the national average."

"It is. Especially at Northern Tier bases, where there
isn't much to keep you busy or active outside the home.
Most of the wives raise children and develop tightly knit
support groups."

"And if you're a career woman?" Erin asked.

"Career wives have an even tougher time," Ty told
her. "They usually don't have children, so they don't
identify with the interests of the majority. Some house-
wives become jealous because the career wife may have
more freedom of self-expression. The situation can lead
to a certain amount of jealousy and uneasiness." A wicked
glint danced in his blue eyes. "You'd make a good military wife."

Erin laughed. "Me? Come on!"

"The marriages that survive do so partly because the
women are strong and self-reliant. You've got those qual-
ities. Plus you've got your own career, which I think
helps a lot in the long run."

John rose, slapping Ty on the back. "I think this young

man just proposed to you, Erin. But if I was in his shoes, I would too! Come on, let's get back to class."

Erin was acutely conscious of heat stealing into her face as Ty pulled out her chair for her to rise. An odd smile quirked one corner of his mouth. The fact that he said nothing to refute John's ridiculous statement made her pulse pound even harder. She rode in uncomfortable silence with both officers back to the Physiology Center.

3

ERIN SPENT ANOTHER hour and a half in the class that afternoon. She was glad when they took a break and Ty wandered back in, handing her a cup of coffee. He perched himself on a chair across from where she was sitting. "Well, did you pay more attention this time?" he inquired.

She produced her notes for his inspection. "I've been very good," she said.

He smiled lazily. "You're like any other Irishwoman," he murmured. "All you need is a guiding hand and you swing right back into line."

"I don't know about that. I take orders from very few people," she disagreed, meeting his challenging gaze. "But after your story on that crewman nearly dying, I was convinced."

"You're intelligent enough to know that," he countered, taking a sip of his own steaming coffee.

"And is that good in your eyes?" she questioned.

"Do you want it to be?"

She colored fiercely. "Why do you have to put everything into personal terms?" she demanded, irritated. Her pulse pounded as a sudden sense of his nearness swept over her.

Ty grinned, enjoying her reaction. "Listen, gal, if we had met under other circumstances, things would be different," he promised huskily.

His words, and the low timbre of his voice, made her feel giddy, and she quickly suppressed the sensation. "And if I didn't know better, I'd suspect the Air Force sent you as a decoy to trick me into writing favorably about them," she retorted.

His expression hardened. "Erin, why do you think the Air Force is so devious?" Abruptly he rose, walking over to the wastebasket and throwing away his empty cup. He turned, his eyes narrowed. "For a writer of nonfiction, you certainly have a creative imagination."

All the hurt and anger that remained in her from Steve's death long ago boiled to the surface in a scalding wave. She rose, her shoulders thrown back, her body rigid. "I wouldn't put anything past the Air Force, Captain! Nothing, do you hear me?" Her trembling voice echoed oddly within the classroom as she faced him. "I keep asking myself why they sent a handsome, very eligible officer to be my escort. Why didn't they send a married officer with five kids? Why you?"

He walked slowly toward her, halting only inches away. His body was rigid with tension and he spoke quietly but with a hint of steel in his voice. "Thanks for the backhanded compliment, but you're wrong, very wrong. By now I should think it would be obvious why they didn't send a married officer to run around with you for two days. They don't get home often enough as it is. The Air Force doesn't want to strain the family ties any more than necessary. So they picked me. I'm divorced. I have no children. I'm on a stand-board crew, which means I don't fly as often as most other SAC crews. Now do you understand?"

Erin felt as if her stomach had fallen to her feet. She took a step away from him, overpowered by his presence. His words had been quiet but spoken with devastating effect. She realized he hadn't wanted to admit any of the personal details about himself, and she felt guilty.

But she had good reason to hate the Air Force. "You can't blame me for taking a jaundiced view," she said through dry lips. "If you were an antimilitary reporter, wouldn't you expect the other party to bend over backward to make things pleasant for you?"

Ty raised his chin, glaring at her. "Lady, you need to be bent over someone's knee and taken to task. In everything you say your hate of the Air Force comes through loud and clear. Why?" He took a step forward, closing the gap between them. "Why?" he demanded again. "Why, Erin? I could deal with you if I knew why. I can respect your reasons. What I can't respect is the hate and anger you're aiming at *me* just because I wear this uniform!"

She made a half turn to escape, but felt the grip of his fingers on her arm bringing her back to face him.

"We're not finished with this conversation, lady."

"Let me go!"

"No. Stand here and take the heat, Erin," he growled. "You owe me an honest answer."

She gritted her teeth, stiffening within his grasp. "You don't deserve to know!" she whispered angrily. Then, to her dismay, tears gathered. She blinked them back furiously. Oh, God, she mustn't cry! What was happening? Every time they were together, it was as if an explosive chemical reaction were taking place.

"Why do you hate me?" he demanded.

A small whimper escaped from her lips. "I don't hate you!" she cried. "Now, let me go!"

Ty released her and stalked toward the door, jerking it open. Halting, he turned. "You're due in the chamber in ten minutes. Be there." The door slammed shut behind him.

Erin stood without moving for long minutes, trying desperately to control the raging emotions Ty had stirred to life. He was right, she had to admit. She hated his uniform, not him. Her eyes grew wide at the realization.

She stared toward the door. She shouldn't feel so drawn to him, but she did. Damn! He had every right to be hurt by her dislike of the Air Force. How would she feel? Groaning, she scooped up her notebook and purse. Right now she had no time to pull him aside and apologize for her overreaction. She would apologize as soon as the hyperbaric chamber experience was completed.

John McIntire smiled genially as she entered the rectangular chamber. Two other airmen, both young, were already outfitted in full oxygen gear. The chamber was empty otherwise, and her footsteps echoed oddly within it.

"Sit here, Erin," McIntire told her. "Let Airman Reeves help you on with the gear." He patted her shoulder in a reassuring gesture. "Don't look so frightened. Everyone goes into this chamber thinking the worst. And you know what? They all come out smiling when it's over. Nothing will happen. You just sit back and relax while Sergeant Calvin and I sit at the controls. You'll be in good hands."

Her heart began a slow pound as an airman in a white helmet with an oxygen mask came forward with her equipment. She didn't like the chamber at all. After fitting on the helmet, she waited while the airman adjusted the oxygen mask. But when it was clapped over her nose and mouth she felt suddenly panicky.

"We have to make sure we have a good seal," the

airman explained, flipping several switches on a console. "If you don't have a good seal, you can get hypoxia in here." He smiled warmly. "And we don't want that to happen. I'm going to shut off the air now. Breathe in as deeply as you can. Next I'll put it on gang load. You'll feel oxygen pressing against your face. At that time I want you to hold your breath so we can make sure there are no leaks between your face and the mask."

Erin barely heard the instructions. Her hands felt cold and clammy. The instant the airman hit the "off" switch, she was without air. Instinctively she gripped the mask, her eyes wide and fearful. The airman nodded as if to indicate that her reaction was normal.

"Good," he praised. "Now for the gang load position."

Air shot through the hose to her mask, and Erin jumped in surprise. The air rushing into the mask bowed the supple plastic of the oxygen mask outward. She tried to breathe normally, but the rush of oxygen continued, and panic surged through her.

"Great," the airman murmured, flipping the switches back to normal. He straightened up and gave the colonel and sergeant who were at the control panel window a thumbs-up gesture. "She's ready," the airman announced.

No, I'm not, Erin screamed silently. She was trembling with fear. Why was she reacting so strongly? Desperately she sought the reason for the ugly backwash of fear coursing through her. It made her feel like a small child who was frightened by a stalking nightmare. She was so caught up in trying to regain her emotional stability that she didn't see Ty Phillips come into the chamber until he passed in front of her. Immediately her panic eased. She was so glad to see him!

With the mask strapped tightly against Ty's face, Erin

couldn't read his features except for his eyes. The anger that had been in them only minutes before was gone. As he sat down beside her, she took a deep steadying breath and closed her eyes.

"Are you all right?" His voice came through the headset in her helmet.

She stared at him. "I—uh, yes. I'm fine." It was difficult to breathe and talk with the mask in place, and remnants of her previous fear still gripped her. Why wouldn't it go away?

Ty was watching her with more than casual interest. Looking up at the airman, he said, "Ask the colonel to take us up nice and slow."

"Yes, sir."

The next instant the hatch clanged shut and a hiss permeated the chamber. To Erin, it sounded as if a huge dungeon door had been slammed shut, imprisoning her inside. She clenched her hands in her lap. Ty reached out, covering her hands with his.

"Take it easy," he soothed. "We'll have to sit here for a half hour while they denitrogenize our blood. That way, when we get to the high altitudes, we won't get the bends."

His words registered but, more than anything, his calming voice worked a minor miracle on her ragged nerves. She closed her eyes. She would just have to sit still for half an hour and talk away the incredible monster of a fear that was eating at her emotional control.

"Right now," Ty murmured, "we're breathing on a demand regulator. That means you have to work a little bit for each breath. I want you to relax some more. You're stiff." He gave her hands a reassuring squeeze. "That's my girl."

Erin saw the corners of his eyes crinkle and knew he

was smiling. It made her feel a little better. He seemed to sense her need to touch him, to hold on to something solid and reassuring. She hadn't realized how tense she'd become, and she forced her shoulders to drop. She tried to inhale more steadily.

"Talk to me," Ty urged gently. "Are you alive and well under that helmet and mask?"

His teasing tone made her smile. Gripping the mask, she nodded. "Barely. . . ."

"This is a real chamber of horrors to most civilians. After a while you'll get used to it. It's a strange sensation and one that very few people except military pilots and crew members experience. Relax, Erin. We'll get you through this in one piece." His eyes took on a familiar glint of mockery. "Besides, I want to take you out to dinner tonight to celebrate passing this test."

She shook her head. "How can you?" she asked in half breaths, again having trouble breathing evenly.

"You think just because we have a tiff I'm going to ignore you? No way, darlin'."

"You're a glutton for punishment then," she told him.

"Maybe, but you're worth the effort."

Erin looked away. Did she dare believe what his words seemed to suggest—that he cared for her a great deal more than she'd realized? Confusion mingled with the gut-wrenching fear that still churned within her. She turned back to him. "Did you have to come in here?" she asked.

He shook his head solemnly. "No. I was watching you through one of the windows and saw you were having a pretty bad reaction. I figured some company might help settle those fears."

Her throat constricted with sudden emotion. "Thanks," was all she could whisper. His fingers tightened against hers. Tentatively she returned the pressure. "I'm glad you're here," she admitted.

His eyes danced with good humor. "There's more than one way to tame a headstrong woman. I feel a little guilty taking advantage of this chamber of horrors to hold your hand. But it's worth it."

The laughter in his voice made the cloak of Erin's dread slip back a bit further from her shoulders. He was a good tonic.

The half hour passed slowly but surely with Ty's easy banter and instructions to keep her mind off her fear. Once their blood was completely free of nitrogen, the steps necessary to familiarize Erin with oxygen at high altitude flight began. She was able to clear her ears simply by swallowing, and Ty gave a thumbs-up signal.

"Hey, pretty good. A lot of people have to do a Valsalva by pinching their noses shut and blowing air back into their eustachian tubes to clear them. Very good, darlin'. Maybe you ought to sign up with the Air Force and become a crew member."

She shook her head firmly. "No, thanks!"

He lifted his broad shoulders, his laughter floating into her ears. "You'd be the prettiest crew member anyone's seen. I can hardly wait to get you up to Sawyer and watch those other crews drool with envy. It isn't every day we get such a good-looking VIP flying with us."

"You're such a crock of blarney, Ty," she accused, smiling in spite of herself.

"Erin, Ty, we're going to take you up to thirty-five thousand feet," McIntire informed them through the microphone.

"Okay," Ty responded. He looked over at her. "At

thirty-five thousand, the mask goes on a pressure-demand position. That means you're going to get a lot of air flowing into it," he explained.

Erin nodded, feeling somewhat easier. So far she had remained in the chamber for forty-five minutes, and the fear seemed to be staying at bay. Again a loud hiss filled the chamber, and Erin instinctively tensed.

The instant the whoosh of oxygen hit her, her fragile control shattered. Suddenly she was drinking in larger and larger drafts of air, unable to exhale. She clawed at the mask, panic surging to the surface. Blackness began to rim her vision, and she shut her eyes.

"Erin!" Ty's voice thundered through the earphone.

She twisted to one side, a cry lodged in her throat. She felt someone's arms go around her, pulling her hand away from the mask. "Exhale!" Ty commanded. "Erin! Listen to me!"

She was aware of sharp orders being given. The two other airmen hovered around her. The hiss of the chamber intensified her fear. Suddenly she was no longer in the chamber, but in the middle of a pond as a twelve-year-old child. She screamed, trying to keep her head above the water that rushed over her. It flowed into her nostrils and down her throat, suffocating her. Wasn't anyone going to help? Was she going to drown? The water kept closing in over her head, and she screamed with panic, her arms flailing wildly.

Then arms came around her, rescuing her. She was being dragged back to shore, gagging and vomiting up the water she'd swallowed. She lay on the bank gasping for air. Someone rolled her over on her stomach and forced the rest of the water out. She lay there for what seemed an eternity, gasping in life-giving oxygen. She had nearly died . . .

Again she felt someone's arms around her. She heard Ty's calming voice. "Inhale just a little, Erin. Come on, that's right. Not a full breath. You aren't going to suffocate. Come on, listen to me." She struggled to concentrate on his words. After a few seconds her vision began to clear and she realized that Ty had his arm around her shoulder, his other hand gripping her hand. Both airmen remained close, their brows drawn together in concern as they watched her. She felt weak and drained.

"Okay, Ty?" McIntire's voice asked.

"Yeah, I think so. Just level us off at twenty-five thousand feet so the oxygen is on demand only," he ordered tightly.

Ty released her slowly, watching her with a guarded expression in his eyes. He didn't relinquish her hand, but gripped it firmly, giving her a measure of solace.

Erin shakily touched her helmet and realized that the mask was back on the demand position, giving her only what she wanted to inhale. Slumping against the seat, she closed her eyes. "I'm—I'm sorry..." she managed, her voice harsh.

"It's all right, darlin'. You regained control. That's all that counts," Ty soothed. "Look, we've got a few other tests to run in here and then we'll be finished." He squeezed her hand. "Think you can stay the distance?"

"As long as you're here," she admitted tiredly, rolling her head to the left, catching his soft blue gaze.

"I'll be here," he promised gently. "Always."

An hour and a half later, Erin walked out of the chamber, still feeling a bit shaken. Ty kept a tight grip on her elbow as he guided her to the lobby. After settling her on one of the leather couches, he went to get some hot coffee. Thanking him, she took the paper cup in her icy fingers. He sat down next to her, his arm resting above her on the couch. Just then John McIntire returned, frowning.

"You okay, Erin?" he asked.

"Fine, John."

"What happened?" He took a chair opposite.

Erin stared dismally down at her lap. "I—I panicked," she admitted hoarsely. "And I feel so stupid."

Ty's hand came to rest on her shoulder. "Don't apologize," he told her. "You'd be surprised to know you aren't the only one who has panicked in there. Right, Colonel?"

McIntire sighed and rubbed his hands along his thighs. "Yes, that's true. Usually they're civilians, Erin. We've seen guys jump up and tear the air hose off the mask trying to get out of there. Some of them have a nasty case of claustrophobia. Others can't take the mask. You've done better than some. Ty and his people will walk you through the mock routine up at Sawyer. Just remember to remain calm and trust the instructions. You've passed the necessary training. I'll have the card for you in just a few minutes, and then Ty will take you back to the hotel to rest."

Erin drew in an unsteady breath, thankful for Ty's closeness. "I feel so tired," she confided.

"That's a very normal reaction," McIntire reassured her. "For about twenty-four hours you're going to feel washed out. Just rest, drink plenty of water or fruit juice, and get some sleep."

"What I need is a drink," she muttered, her nerves raw.

McIntire rose, grinning. "Take a drink now and you'll be higher than a kite. The chamber experience makes drinking alcoholic beverages off limits for at least a day.

Stick with Ty and he'll help you readjust through this uncomfortable period." After giving her another reassuring pat on the back, he left them.

Erin placed her coffee cup on the table and buried her head in her hands. "I feel like such an utter fool, Ty."

"Come on, let's get you back to the hotel," he urged, standing. He took her arm, helping her to her feet. "I'll come back later and pick up the paperwork for you," he murmured.

The sun was shining brightly and the wind caressed Erin's face as they walked to the car. She relished walking out into the sunlight, away from the sterile atmosphere of the chamber. Ty opened the car door for her and she slid in. The interior was warm and helped take away the last of her chill. Ty got in and glanced over at her, worry still creasing his face. "Maybe it would help to cry," he observed soberly.

Erin lifted her chin to look at him, her lips parted and trembling at the husky tenor of his voice. His concern seemed so genuine. Tears welled, and she choked back a sob. "I—I almost drowned when I was twelve, Ty. That—that horrible chamber brought it all back." Suddenly she was sobbing uncontrollably. She heard him call her name, felt his arms going around her. Making no effort to stop him, she fell against his strong lean body, and cried into his shoulder.

He soothed her with gentle words, tenderly stroking her hair. "My proud Irish lady," he whispered, "don't ever be afraid to cry." He embraced her more tightly for a moment and then placed his fingers lightly beneath her chin, forcing her to meet his gaze. She felt tears streaming down her glistening cheeks as she opened her eyes. "Don't ever be ashamed of crying, Erin. Most women can cry easily. What happened to you, my beautiful banshee witch?" He smiled tenderly, searching her upturned face. "Maybe it's because you have dark hair instead of red hair." He released her chin and brushed the tears from her cheeks.

Her heart soared with each feather-light graze of his hand against her skin. A growing warmth uncoiled within her, and she continued to drink in his mesmerizing gaze. Her lips parted, and he frowned. Time seemed to hang suspended between them; the stillness felt magnified to a painful level. She was resting against his lean body, intensely aware of him as a man.

His arm tightened around her shoulder, and he groaned her name softly, pulling her forward. She closed her eyes, leaning up to meet his strong mouth. She craved his touch. It brought her dormant desires to life and left her weak with need.

His mouth brushed her lips, tasting them, testing them. She sighed and relaxed within his arms, her hand curving instinctively around his neck. His mouth molded strongly against her lips, parting them, seeking entrance. His rough cheek against her flesh sent prickles of delight through her body. His breath, warm and moist, heightened her senses. His mouth moved against her lips, demanding yet gentle. It was a deep, long kiss, one of tentative sensitive exploration.

Erin responded hungrily, instinctively realizing that Ty cared deeply for her. He wasn't like many other men she knew. He played for keeps, not for a one-night stand or a brief fling. And in sensing that, Erin entrusted herself to him on a deep, elemental level.

He broke contact with her mouth and studied her carefully, as if memorizing her upturned features. "I don't want to stop," he admitted thickly. He brushed her cheek with strong fingers and forced a slight smile to his lips. "You're heady stuff, lady."

Focusing on the fires burning brightly within her body, she couldn't speak. She had never been kissed so thoroughly, so poignantly. It was as if he had put his whole heart and soul into that one act. In the past men had plundered her lips, almost assaulting her in a vain effort to convey their passion. But not Ty. Erin gazed somberly up at him, meeting his cobalt eyes. He had kissed her gently, with due respect for her needs and desires. What had he said before? That all she needed was a coaxing hand? His kiss had been coaxing, a sharing between them. It had been filled with silent promises. Erin trembled inwardly, thinking of those thrilling promises.

She pulled away, unable to meet his curious, probing gaze any longer. Lowering her lashes, she murmured, "Please, take me back to the hotel."

Ty sighed and leaned back, placing his hands on the steering wheel. "I'd *like* to take you home with me."

She gasped and jerked her head up. He was serious. Pain twisted through her.

"I'm thirty-two years old, Erin," he said quietly, "and I learned a long time ago to be honest with women. It's been a long time since anyone has affected me like you do."

His husky voice vibrated with feeling, leaving her uncomfortable and excited at the same time. "You barely know me," she whispered.

He scowled, watching her. "But I know myself. And I know what you're doing to me." He pursed his mouth, staring stright ahead, the minutes stretching by in tense silence.

"When I was handed this assignment, I complained

a lot. I no more wanted to escort some antimilitary reporter around than take on a thirty-hour mission. And when I was told you were a woman, I damn near told the colonel to take his friendly suggestion and shove it. Now"—he sighed and glanced over at her—"my whole world has come to a stop. When I saw you getting off the plane, I thought how beautiful you were from a distance. I liked the way you walked with confidence. I like a woman who can stand on her own two feet and meet the world on her own terms. When you turned around, I damn near forgot everything—my reason for being there, everything. I was mesmerized by your blue eyes. Then when I sensed your immediate hatred of me and the Air Force, I was stunned." He shrugged helplessly. "I'm not really in the habit of facing off with a woman like I did with you, Erin. But the strength of your antagonism brought out the side of me that has to fight back."

She clenched her hands tightly in her lap, her heart racing painfully. "I have a lot to apologize for, Ty," she admitted hoarsely.

"I'm not telling you this to get an apology out of you, darlin'. I just want you to know where you stand with me. It may mean nothing to you." He gave a mirthless laugh. "Hell, it could be totally one-sided. But the way you kissed me back..." His voice dropped to a rough whisper. "Damn, this is crazy. I want you to know I didn't come down here intending to fall for you, Erin. It was the farthest thing from my mind. God knows I've got enough to worry about already with my duties with SAC. Escorting you was supposed to be a brief chore, rotten duty at best." He shook his head, staring pensively out the window. "This wasn't supposed to happen."

She managed a rueful smile. "You're right."

"Reality isn't built on supposed-to-be's."

"Right again."

"Look, Erin, you've been through plenty today without me laying my confessions on your doorstep. You look like you could use some sleep."

She nodded, her mind fuzzy with exhaustion and her heart throbbing with a sweet aching pain. Laying her head back against the seat, she closed her eyes. Within minutes she had slipped into a deep sleep.

Hearing her name being called, she moaned softly. Ty's hand lingered on her shoulder, and he gave her another gentle shake.

"We're here, Erin," he said softly. "I'd carry you in, but I'm afraid it would cause quite a stir."

She forced her eyes open and sat up. Her dark hair spilled forward as she forced herself awake. "That's all right," she murmured huskily, her voice thick with sleep. "Just guide me in the general direction of my room. I'm so tired."

"I know. Come on, I'll do better than that."

He helped her from the car, his arm sliding around her waist. She leaned gratefully against him, content to be within his embrace. He opened the door to her room and guided her to the bed. Leaving her sitting on the edge, he moved to the large windows and pulled the curtains closed. "Take your shoes off," he said.

Erin did as she was ordered, then pulled herself up on the bed and lay down. Exhaustion claimed her, and she closed her eyes. Somewhere in the back of her mind she heard him open and close a closet door. Vaguely she felt a blanket being thrown across her. He tucked it in around her shoulders and briefly stroked her hair.

"Go to sleep, darlin'," he urged softly. It was the last thing she remembered before spiraling into the darkness.

4

ERIN AWOKE NEAR six the next morning. Feeling disoriented and uncomfortable from sleeping in her clothes, she opted for a hot bath to soak away her remaining fatigue. She changed into designer jeans and a silk blouse of pale apricot and brushed her hair vigorously until it shone. At last she felt ready to face the world. The phone rang at eight.

"How do you feel after yesterday?" Ty asked.

A smile curved her lips, and she sat down on the edge of the bed, cradling the receiver against her ear. "Like I still have a hangover. It would be one thing if I'd caroused all night and deserved this agony."

Ty laughed gently. "Going through the chamber is always rough."

"Why didn't somebody tell me that before?"

"What? And drag you into it kicking and screaming? No way. I tangled with you once, remember?"

"We'll just have to call a truce," she said amiably.

"Great. How about breakfast? Are you hungry?"

"Starving."

"Good. I'll come by and pick you up. It'll be just a few minutes."

Erin replaced the receiver and stared at it for a long time. She was buoyant. Before Ty called, she had felt listless. Frowning, she rose slowly to her full height of five-eight. His voice had been warm and caressing over the phone, creating a sensuous tension between them, which she had responded to like a flower to sunshine.

After putting on a light dash of burgundy lipstick, she took stock of herself in the mirror.

She rarely took great pains with her appearance, but today she looked different, prettier. The image that stared back was one of a woman in her maturity. Even in jeans she looked elegantly sleek, the raw-silk blouse complementing her dusky-peach skin. Studying herself more closely, she noticed an extra sparkle dancing in the depths of her turquoise eyes. Ty had put that there.

At a light knock on the door, she went to open it after picking up her purse and a suede blazer. Ty's open admiration made her feel like a giddy schoolgirl. He stood in the doorway in jeans and a pale-blue short-sleeved shirt, his hands resting easily on his slim hips. "Lady, you are going to cause a riot up at Sawyer," he said, his pleased gaze traveling the length of her body.

Erin laughed, feeling the heat of a blush sweep across her neck and face. "Me? Look at you! I don't believe it. You look like a civilian!"

He grinned recklessly and helped her on with the blazer. As he drew her long hair from beneath the jacket, his fingers brushed against her neck. Her skin prickled pleasurably. He allowed the thick mane to cascade across her shoulders. "Beautiful hair," he murmured, his hands resting lightly against her arms. He leaned closer and breathed in deeply. "You smell like a bouquet of flowers."

"You're awfully romantic today, Captain Phillips,"

she returned lightly, though her pulse was racing. "Doesn't that go against the image you usually project?" She left his embrace, turning and smiling up at him. He looked boyish and relaxed this morning.

He placed his hand in the small of her back and guided her toward the elevator. "Somewhere in between the two extremes is my reality, Erin." He was suddenly serious. "We're constantly training. Buff crews never get a break. We eat, live, sleep, and fly together as a unit. Maybe ten days out of the month, the guys get to go home to their wives and kids." He paused. "We live for the Organizational Readiness Inspection, and we have so many other tests to do besides that . . ." He shook his head. "If we aren't being tested for our particular skills, we're studying our fool heads off on new systems procedures and other complicated modes of operation."

The elevator doors opened, and he ushered her in. She stayed close to him, wanting to be near his lean male strength. She noticed his arms—they hadn't an extra ounce of flesh. The play of muscles in them suggested that he either worked out with weights or that flying the Buff was much more physically demanding than she'd thought. As they padded down the carpeted hall toward the restaurant, she said, "I did want to know more about a Buff pilot's life-style."

Ty smiled lazily. "Believe me, if we find anyone who's willing to listen, we'll bend your ear." He asked the dining room hostess to show them to a table near a window. Once they were seated, he ordered coffee for both of them.

"I guess reporters live on coffee just like we do," he said.

Erin nodded. "I heard you and John McIntire discussing the pros and cons of having a beer after a mission," she said.

"Just wait and see, darlin'. After the mission, you'll be heading to the refrigerator we have at the squadron just like the rest of us," he promised, taking a sip of coffee.

"Why beer?" she asked.

"It releases you. After a ten- or twelve-hour mission, where you're up at thirty-nine thousand and down on the deck at three hundred feet, you feel completely sapped. A beer after a mission seems to get rid of that fatigue and helps us relax."

The waitress hovered nearby. Ty ordered for them and returned his full attention to Erin. His mood turned serious. "Are you due to take the noon flight back to New York?"

She nodded, realizing all at once that she didn't want to go. The thought stunned her, and she carefully set down her coffee cup. Ty Phillips seemed to wield some sort of emotional magic. Her stomach knotted, and she forced a smile she didn't feel. "Yes, I'll have to assemble all my notes and read through the rest of the literature that's waiting for me back at my office."

Ty picked up a fork and moved it around on the tablecloth in a distracted motion. "You'll love the Upper Peninsula in October. Matter of fact, the autumn colors will be in full swing by the time you arrive." He glanced up at her. "Ever been out in the country much?"

She rested her chin against her folded hands. "No, I'm a city girl through and through. And what's the Upper Peninsula?"

"The upper half of Michigan. Too bad you aren't driving up. You would cross the Mackinac Bridge, which connects lower and upper Michigan. It's a beautiful bridge, and the view across the lakes is fantastic."

"I think you Buff pilots see all things made of metal as beautiful," she teased.

A slow smile brightened his expression. "What I see right now is breathtaking," he murmured, meeting and catching her startled glance.

She tried to recover from his compliment. "If all Buff pilots are as silver-tongued as you are, I'm in trouble." She laughed.

He reached over, capturing her arm in a caressing gesture. "Take the compliment and say thank you, Erin."

She colored fiercely. "You're making me uncomfortable, Ty."

"Good. I can see you haven't been getting your share of compliments lately. What's the matter with the guys back in the city?"

"Maybe they aren't like Buff crews, who live in isolated areas and never see women," she teased back.

Ty nodded. "You got that right. The Upper Peninsula isn't exactly crowded with people. Most of the women up there are married."

"Sounds like a chronic problem," she agreed.

"That's why most Buff crew members are married or get married pretty quickly. Going to a Norther Tier means being deprived of most outside activities, such as those you can usually find near a large city. It gets damn lonely, but sharing it with a wife and kids helps a lot."

"You were married," Erin blurted out, then gasped, stunned that she had broached such a personal subject. She held her breath, watching his face. A corner of his mouth pulled in, as if he felt a twinge of pain. Finally he looked up, holding her widened gaze. "I'm sorry," she said quickly. "I didn't mean——"

"That's all right," he interrupted. He leaned back, his expression thoughtful. "Anne never adjusted to military life. She and I were married when I graduated from flight training. She was twenty-three at the time. Looking back on it, I can see that she was immature for her age. She had been overly protected by her parents, who were civilians. I requested Buff duty because it's considered good background for attaining rank later on. My first assignment was at Minot, North Dakota." He shrugged. "When you take a southern woman who has never seen snow or experienced temperatures of thirty degrees below zero, and then take her husband away for days on end ... well, you end up with a strained relationship," he explained.

"I can see that," Erin murmured, feeling sudden compassion for his ex-wife. "Do many women without a military background have trouble adjusting?" she asked.

Ty took a deep steadying breath. "You'd better believe it. They either adjust quickly or the marriage dies. There's no in between. If you marry an officer, you've just acquired the Air Force as a mother-in-law. Anne and I faced the usual tensions. I was a young lieutenant trying to get ahead, and I took on extra duties. I'd come home with my work and, although I tried to divide my time between the job and Anne, our relationship started falling apart."

"It doesn't seem fair to the woman," Erin said, frowning.

"It isn't," he agreed soberly.

"But she tried?"

Ty nodded. "Yes, we both did. The final split came when I got the promotion I wanted and was assigned to other extra duty. You see, there's a real problem in the SAC ranking system, Erin. The idea is not just to fly and remain a lieutenant or captain forever. In SAC everyone is highly trained. We're all about the same in caliber and quality. There's nothing that sets us apart from one another. So we end up taking on extra duties to shine, if you will, and be noticed for the next promotion."

"It sounds like a rough way to live."

"For the women and children, it is. Being a military wife, in my mind, is one of the most demanding jobs in the world. Not only do they have to adjust to military life, but also their husbands are gone a great deal of the time flying long missions. They come home absolutely exhausted. I can remember times when I'd fly a sixteen-hour flight, come home, and sleep for ten hours. Naturally Anne would want to see me, talk to me, tell me what had gone right or wrong in my absence. I couldn't keep my eyes open. She felt shut out, abandoned." His expression became troubled. "A military wife either develops a backbone of steel and plenty of independence or she breaks under the system."

"And Anne broke?"

"Yes. It broke me too. I loved her." He sat up, resting his elbows on the table. "That was six years ago. The pain has gone with time. But I learned from the experience," he observed wryly.

Erin remembered her own pain, the bitterness she still felt toward the Air Force for allowing her husband to be killed. "Yes," she answered softly, "I know all about that too."

The waitress brought their orders, and they ate in silence. Erin chastised herself for broaching the subject of Ty's broken marriage. He didn't strike her as a man who would give up easily on something he loved or cared about. She wondered if Anne had truly tried to adjust. Perhaps her immaturity had been as responsible for the breakup as Ty's determination to pursue a career in the military. It seemed that Ty would never put the blame on Anne's shoulders. Instead he had stacked the evidence against himself. His fairness and consideration made her feel warm all over.

After the dishes had been cleared away, Ty continued the conversation. "I want to ask you a very personal question, Erin," he said. "And if you want to tell me that it's none of my business, I'll understand."

Her heart squeezed as she stared across the table at him. His tone was probing, but gentle. She knew she couldn't refuse him and she lowered her gaze. "I know what you're going to ask."

"I don't want to know out of idle curiosity, if that makes it any easier for you," he murmured.

She chewed on her lower lip. Finally she raised her head, meeting his concerned gaze. He was bestowing the same indefinable warmth and care on her that he had shown for Anne. The realization made it easier to share with him. "I'm not a stranger to the military world, Ty," she admitted, her voice barely above a whisper. "I got married right out of high school to Steven Rosen. He had just come out of army officers' school, and we were assigned to a large base in California." She knotted the napkin in her lap. "I was hopelessly in love with him. At eighteen I was a starry-eyed romantic and very idealistic." She forced a smile. "It wasn't a very good combination."

"But there's nothing wrong with it, either," Ty returned.

"It didn't help, in my case. Steve was doing a lot of flying out of Travis Air Force Base with the C-130's at that time."

Ty drew in a sharp breath. "Don't tell me he died in a crash."

A knot formed in Erin's throat. "Yes. Yes, he did. I was twenty years old when it happened. They found out later that it was pilot error. It—it made it all the harder to bear, Ty."

"What a rotten thing to happen," he growled. He looked at her keenly, his blue eyes narrowing with intensity. "You had every reason to hate the way you did, Erin."

"No, not really. Like I said," she murmured, taking an unsteady gulp of air, "I was young, naive, and idealistic. Having Steve torn from me scarred my heart for a long, long time afterward. But looking back on it, I wonder if our marriage would have lasted. Even at eighteen I felt a strong need to pursue my own career. Steve didn't understand why I needed to be outside the house. He was often angry at me."

"He was a chauvinist?" Ty asked gently.

"Yes. Frankly, I don't think his male ego could have dealt with another breadwinner in the family. But at that age I didn't realize what some of the implications were for a few years from then. During the two years of our marriage I went to college and worked toward a degree in journalism."

"Steve sounds like an aggressive type of military officer," Ty observed.

"He wasn't only militarily inclined, Ty; he was militaristic. His bearing, manner, and intelligence won him the immediate respect of his superiors. That's why they were grooming him for higher rank. He was a golden boy of sorts."

Ty shook his head ruefully. "I would never have thought that you and I had similar pasts."

"I know," she murmured, feeling emotionally drained.

"So when you got this assignment, it was like re-opening old wounds."

Erin nodded. "Yes. I tried to get out of it. But if I do a good job, I may get a promotion. I'm tired of traveling all over the country for stories. I'd like to stay put for a while."

He smiled. "Just for a while, darlin'. You'll always enjoy your work, but maybe in a different capacity."

She agreed. "Maybe I'm just tired."

"You know, coming up to Sawyer could be a little vacation for you."

"How?"

His gaze grew intimate. "According to the itinerary you'll stay at the distinguished visitors' quarters. However, I just happen to live off base in a beautiful wooded area south of Marquette. There's plenty of room to hike and picnic. Strictly a personal invitation, you understand, for an afternoon. The Air Force would probably frown on our spending time together, but that's their problem. What do you say?"

She broke into a broad smile. "It sounds wonderful!"

"Great. We'll take half a day off from your grueling schedule before the Buff flight and play hooky. That ought to put that poor public affairs lieutenant into a tailspin."

"I'll call him and ask for a lighter schedule. That way I won't be stepping on any feet or causing hard feelings."

"Do that. Besides, who said all work and no play is good?"

"Not me," Erin said, suddenly aware of an overwhelming happiness.

Ty glanced at his watch. "It's about that time, gal. We'd best get a move on or you'll miss your flight." He flashed her a smile as he rose. "An Army wife," he teased gently. "I'll never let you live it down."

She stood, following him out of the dining room, feeling freer than she had in a long time. His teasing about her past no longer bothered her. Maybe the simple act of talking to someone who understood the situation she'd been in and the pain she'd faced had helped to finally heal the old wound. Ty opened the door for her and casually draped his arm around her shoulders, drawing her near.

"I'm going to miss you," he whispered fiercely.

Erin's arm went around his lean waist. "It's been good meeting you too, Captain Phillips," she baited, smiling up at him.

"You're heady stuff, gal. I'm going to need a month to recover from this encounter. You're worse than a magnetic storm to my gyro."

Erin laughed at his ridiculous metaphor. "Spoken like a true Buff pilot," she told him. Their words were light, but underneath she knew they would miss each other.

The thought made her feel panic as well as joy. She felt protected within his arms, intensely aware of his strength of body and character. He had shortened his stride for her sake and she was grateful. She hoped to keep their parting light.

Suddenly her life seemed to be spiraling into a tailspin. Where was she going? What was happening? How did Ty fit into the larger picture of her life? Or did he? Icy waters of reality seemed to have been thrown over her ebullient mood. She was walking with an incredibly handsome man with attributes that struck responsive chords deep within her. But he wore an Air Force uniform, and his career was a demanding, brutal mistress. Some of her happiness ebbed away. Seeming to sense it, Ty gave her a gentle embrace.

"Something wrong?"

She glanced guiltily up at him. "No," she lied.

"You were walking on air a moment ago," he observed, studying her.

She squirmed beneath his radar-sharp gaze. "Stop being so damn perceptive!" she accused in a teasing voice.

"Hmmm, my Irishwoman has gone moody on me now."

"You, of all people, shouldn't be surprised."

He grinned boyishly. "I'm not. And never will be. That's another thing I like about you, Erin Quinlan. You make no excuse for how you feel, from one quicksilver moment to another. It makes you a provocative, fascinating creature." His voice had sunk to a husky whisper.

"In your eyes only," she contradicted, embarrassed by his words.

He leaned over and placed a quick kiss on her hair. "That's all that counts, darlin'. Come on, let's get your luggage and meet that plane."

They didn't say much after dispensing with her luggage and getting her boarding pass for the flight. What *was* there to say?

Erin dreaded hearing the call to board. Ty lounged beside her like a lion lazing in the late afternoon sun. She smiled secretly, amazed at how youthful he looked out of uniform. His lean, muscular legs were spread before him, and he seemed poured into the lounge chair.

Several times she opened her mouth to speak and bit back the words, afraid of his recrimination, which might follow. Had two days gone by? It seemed as if they had known each other forever.

He had sobered greatly since coming to the airport. Was he going to miss her? What did she mean to him? Again the urge to ask him almost made her speak, but she gripped her purse and stared down at it, fighting back the temptation to force him to say things he might not be ready to say.

Just then the ticket agent announced the boarding. Almost simultaneously Erin felt Ty's reassuring fingers sliding down her wrist, capturing her hand firmly. She looked up at him. Suddenly it was too late to say the things she needed desperately to tell him. He offered her a tender smile.

"Come on, my beautiful banshee. Let's get you aboard so your editor doesn't have cardiac arrest wondering why you don't show up on time."

Erin rose, glad that he still held her hand. "Don't worry, he wouldn't have a heart attack," she said. "Just as long as the article meets the deadline at the end of November, he won't care where I am." She cringed inwardly. Good Lord! What suggestions was she making?

Ty watched her with an unreadable expression. "You might not get in hot water, but I would. If I don't show up at K. I. Siberia tonight, all hell will break loose."

She gave a little laugh. "K. I. Siberia? Is that what you fondly call your air base?"

"Yup. We get two hundred and ten inches of snow each year. I've taken up snow sports in defense. A lot of the guys hate the Northern Tier bases because they're so desolate and isolated."

"You don't seem to mind."

"No. I learned to ski and ice fish." He grinned and

pulled her to a halt. "That's better, gal. You look so damn tempting when you smile." He reached out, brushing a strand of hair from her cheek. His face became serious and his eyes grew dark as he looked down at her. It was as if he were trying to keep her in his mind forever. "But I'll tell you," he added, his hands coming to rest on her shoulders, "if anything or anyone could entice me not to show up at base, it would be you, darlin'."

She tried to muster a smile for both of them, but her heart twisted with sadness. Ty had affected her so deeply in such a short time that she felt the anguish of their parting keenly. Her inner struggle must have shown in her eyes because Ty gave her a small shake.

"You got a boyfriend waiting to pick you up at La Guardia?" he asked.

She gave him a shocked look and blurted out, "Why— no!"

"Hmm. That's good for a start. What about a steady guy waiting to see you come back to the big city?"

She managed an embarrassed laugh. "Really, Ty! What if there is?"

His eyes darkened to a cobalt blue and a grim smile hovered around his sensual mouth. "If you do, gal, then he's got some heavy competition on his hands. You tell him that for me."

"Do all you bomber pilots go around threatening men whose women you want?" she demanded, caught up in his teasing.

"We got a few sayings for bomber pilots," he agreed gravely. "You might want to pass them on to him just in case."

"Okay," she returned just as gravely, matching his droll expression.

"One is—you've gotta be tough to fly the heavies. The other is—tough enough to fly the Buff. Either one will suffice. He'll get the message."

She grinned. "My, my. You bomber pilots play for keeps, don't you?"

Ty guided her toward the corridor leading down to the plane. "We aren't like fighter jockeys, who get frontal lobotomies to fly those hotshot aircraft, darlin'. We take our time, watch, weigh, and measure everything before we move in. But once we do, it's for keeps." His words seemed both a promise and a threat.

She halted, turning and facing him, amazed by his ability to lift her flagging spirits. "One thing for sure, Captain Phillips, I've completely reevaluated bomber pilots. They aren't stupid, slow, or slothful. Instead, I think you're all dominating, manipulative, and shrewd!"

Ty laughed heartily. "I'm not sure I want to trade one for the other." He stared down at her, his smile fading. "Give me a hug and then do an about-face and get on that plane. Otherwise, I'm not going to be responsible for my actions," he ordered huskily.

It was so easy to fall into his arms and allow his lean male body to support her completely. His arms tightened around her, and she rested her head against his shoulder for a brief moment. Her heart was hammering painfully in her breast. At that instant she didn't want to leave him. He pushed her gently away, a tender smile on his mouth, one that did not reach his eyes. "I'll see you in a month," he promised, giving her a nudge toward the ramp.

She hesitated only an instant, nodded, and then turned, walking quickly away. She didn't dare look back for fear she wouldn't be able to leave him after all.

Once settled on the plane, she laid her head back against the seat and closed her eyes. Taking a deep breath, she catalogued her emotions—euphoria, excitement, sadness, and fright. Shakily she pushed her dark hair away from her face, trying desperately to think rationally and with logic. Ty Phillips was far too mesmerizing for her own good!

5

ERIN WAS SIFTING through the information the Air Force had sent her on the Strategic Air Command. For the tenth time that morning she looked out across the New York skyline and imagined the autumn leaves, which must be turning beautiful colors by now up in Michigan. She sighed softly and ran slender fingers across the pamphlets and brochures. It had been almost three weeks since she'd left Ty Phillips at the Dayton Airport. Yet neither of them had wanted her to leave. She grimaced, resting her chin in her palm and staring dreamily out the window. The cirrus clouds floating in a blue sky looked like the mane of a horse flowing in the wind.

How many times had she wondered if Ty was flying his Buff over the Atlantic Seaboard? Each time she saw contrails high in the sky, she thought of him. Dejectedly she forced herself back to work, back to sifting through the huge piles of literature she had amassed in an effort to find the facts to support the angle Bruce demanded she take in her article.

Since returning to New York, she had begun to take stock of her emotions. What did she want from life? Something was missing, something that clamored more strongly than ever to be heard and recognized. Ty Phillips had forced her to look inward and account for herself.

She had thought that, with time and distance, the memory of him would fade. But it was just as easy to conjure up his laughter or his mirthful expression today as it had been weeks before. She had replayed their conversations many times in her head, seeking to know more, to understand more clearly the enigmatic officer.

"Erin!" her secretary, Ruth Adams, called excitedly. She hurried into Erin's office, her eyes glowing. "Look at this! It just arrived for you. Can you believe it?" Ruth moved aside, her hands clasped in delight as a florist entered the office and placed a huge bouquet of bird-of-paradise on the corner of Erin's desk. Smiling, the young man pulled an envelope from his jacket.

"You're Miss Erin Quinlan?"

She flushed, staring at the gorgeous rare flowers. Their bright-orange and purple color made her think again of autumn leaves. "Yes, I am," she murmured.

"Oh!" Ruth cried, standing over them. "Aren't they beautiful! Do you realize how much these cost?"

Erin smiled, taking the envelope from the florist's hand. He grinned bashfully, meeting her gaze. "I took the order," he said, a note of pride in his voice.

Her hand shook imperceptibly as she ran her fingers along the stiff paper. "Thank you. They're beautiful."

"Yes, ma'am." He dipped his head and added shyly, "You must be awful special."

Erin tilted her head. "Oh?"

"Yes, ma'am. He called from, ah—let's see. . . . Oh, yeah, a place I can't even say right."

Her heart leaped. "Go on."

The florist scratched his head. "Some strange-sounding place in Australia."

Erin inhaled sharply; Ruth gasped openly. "Australia?" Erin echoed, looking at the envelope.

"Yes, ma'am. We had a terrible phone connection. He kept repeating the message, and I kept getting only bits and pieces of it." He flushed scarlet. "He must think a whole lot of you to call all the way from there, much less spend twenty minutes on the phone gettin' that letter to you. Hope you enjoy them," he called, and disappeared out the door.

Ruth clasped her hands to her breast, peering over the bouquet at Erin. "What a beautiful gesture." She sighed. "Who is it? He must be a romantic. Just think, he called all the way from Australia."

"Ruth, don't you have that article—"

Her secretary laughed gaily. "Okay, I get the hint! I'll shut the door to make sure you have absolute privacy as you read that letter."

Erin smiled and shook her head, watching her secretary leave. Silence settled around her, and she gazed up at the bird-of-paradise. She gently eased the envelope open. It had been painstakingly typed; several blotches of white erasure liquid were visible. A warm smile pulled at her lips as her gaze fell on the signature—"Ty." Leaning back in her leather chair, she held the crisp letter in both hands.

Dear Erin:

Take my word for it, the leaves are turning up at K. I. Sawyer. They've had us on a secret mission since my return, so I couldn't contact you at all until just now. I thought the bird-of-paradise best symbolized an aircraft—or maybe the colors here in the Upper Peninsula. I'll meet you at the Marquette Airport on the 20th. I've got the picnic basket packed. All I need is you.

Ty.

She took a long, unsteady breath, allowing a growing warmth to fill her totally. Resting the letter against her breast, she looked over at the flowers. He was right— their arrow-shaped heads did look like aircraft with wings. She smiled wistfully, appreciating his thoughtful gesture.

She had tried to ignore the fact that, since her return, she hadn't heard one word from him. At first she had been crushed, then logic had rescued her. What she had felt toward Ty was simply infatuation, fleeting at best.

But was it really only that? He had been away on a long mission, which explained his failure to communicate sooner. She reread the letter four times and finally forced herself to get back to work.

An hour later, Bruce, her editor, knocked and sauntered in. He took the pipe from his mouth and his eyebrows shot upward in surprise at the sight of the flowers on her desk. "I heard Ruth raving about the bird-of-paradise you just got from a secret admirer in Australia." He ambled over, studying them critically, then glanced at her out of the corner of his eye. "Must be a very rich secret admirer."

She tucked Ty's letter in the top drawer of her desk and shut it gently, not wanting him to notice. "They're from Captain Phillips, Bruce."

"Ah," he said, his brows moving upward again. He sucked noisily on the pipe and then tamped it down methodically. "So, the Air Force is using him to butter you up so you'll write a less negative article, huh?"

Erin frowned at his suggestion. Bruce had been bothering her constantly about the article. She had known him to behave similarly with other reporters when an important article was in the making. Now it was her turn. "I don't think so," she said, reluctant to discuss the personal nature of her relationship with Ty.

Bruce watched her closely, relighting his pipe. A cloud of blue-gray smoke drifted around his head. "Do I detect a note of irritation in your voice?" he asked snidely.

She stood up restlessly. "You do." She turned to him. "We can't be paranoid about this, Bruce. At first I was; I'm not now." She gestured toward the flowers. "I think Captain Phillips probably felt bad about not contacting me for three weeks. He mentioned in his note that he plans to pick me up at Marquette Airport, nothing more. Just business." At Bruce's skeptical expression, her resentment increased.

He continued to puff nonchalantly on his pipe. "Maybe we are a little paranoid." He shifted, smiling in a way that she knew was intended to threaten her. He gestured toward the literature on her desk. "Looks like you've been going over all that information. What have you found to support the publisher's view?"

Erin breathed a sigh of relief, glad to get onto a safer subject. She sat back down in her chair. "You want the honest truth?"

"Of course."

"Not much. If we take out the bomber wing, we have two types of missiles with which to defend our country, and neither can be recalled from a target once it's set in motion."

"But the B-1 B bomber is going to cost us as much as twenty billion dollars. How can you justify that?"

Erin pulled out her notes. "*If* the Air Force keeps the Buff—I mean, the B-52's—flying until the end of this century, it will cost upwards of ninety-two billion dollars to keep refitting them. So what's the better buy here?" she challenged.

Bruce gave her a slightly irritated look. "Give me reasons we should keep any bombers, Erin."

"First, you have to understand SAC's entire concept of the Triad, Bruce. SAC feels that flexibility is the key to our strategic and tactical forces. Second, we can only ensure the survival of manned bombers. These bombers can be redirected or recalled with absolute confidence. Let's say an unfriendly nation threatens us. In all probability SAC would lift off a certain number of bombers. Captain Phillips mentioned that they go out to preset coordinates and fly a pattern, waiting for further commands. If they're in the air long enough, they're refueled by KC-135 tankers. Therefore, they can act as a threat, to help deescalate a situation."

He snorted contemptuously. "Or escalate it, as the case may be."

Erin shrugged. "SAC has been around since World War Two, and so far, no nuclear wars. They might be doing something right."

"I doubt it," he said, beginning to pace in front of her desk, puffing intently on his pipe. "Look at the mess the world's in now."

Her patience lessened. "Bruce, we can't blame SAC for aggression all over the world! Are you trying to use SAC as a scapegoat?"

He turned, frowning. "Ian Wright, the publisher, has strong ties to Washington. He's antidefense. Several lobbying groups and liberal senators feel that the B-1 B program and B-52 refurbishing plan are a waste of money."

Erin pursed her lips, clamping down on her rising

temper. "Then you don't want a factual article on SAC?" she challenged.

They stared at each other in silence. Finally Bruce sighed and shook his head. "Look," he said, "all the facts aren't in yet. You still have to go to Sawyer. See what you can find out there."

"And when I do, Bruce, what if the facts still fall in favor of retaining a bomber in the Triad?" she asked tightly. He had never asked her to lie in an article, or even to hold a position that went against her conscience. If he wanted a biased article, he should write it himself. It was beneath her professional dignity to do it for him, and he knew it.

"Let's just wait and see, Erin." He halted at the door. "You make a pretty good case for the B-1 B. If I didn't know better, I'd say the Air Force had somehow brainwashed you."

"No one buys me," she stated calmly, daring him to say one more word against her.

"I didn't mean to imply that, Erin. Sorry; it's just that Ian is really pressuring me for this article and ..." He left his sentence unfinished, waved at her, and left the office.

She sat down, exhausted, and glanced at the material surrounding her and at the flowers. The information Bruce had supplied her with was blatantly anti-Air Force. But what of the Air Force material? As Bruce had suggested, was she being bought? Was all her information slanted in favor of the B-52 and B-1 B? And how much had Ty influenced her?

She recalled what her opinions had been before she'd met him. She'd been just as anxious to attack SAC in print as Bruce still was. But then she had met a bomber pilot, a man who was unique, no matter who she compared him to. Were the men of SAC all like Ty? Did they all have a similar idealism? A belief that they contributed to keeping peace in the world by providing a deterrent? Rubbing her face wearily, she decided to call it a day and go home.

Then an idea struck her, and on an impulse she called a friend of hers. "Lisa, I want to take you up on that invitation to use your cabin in the Catskills. Is it going to be available this weekend?"

"Sure! It's about time you left the city and got some good earth beneath your feet." Lisa laughed. "Just remember, the key is under the rubber mat on the porch."

Erin smiled, already feeling a pressing weight being lifted from her shoulders. "Great!"

"The cabin's stocked, but you'll need to buy perishables. And if you want wine, better take some along."

"I will. I need some time alone to think," she confided.

"Well, enjoy! I'll call you Monday morning to see if you got back to the city all right."

Erin laughed. "Don't worry, I will. Thanks, Lisa. I owe you one."

She hung up and stared blankly at the opposite wall. Why was she going up to a cabin in the mountains now? Lisa had been offering her the cabin for the last two years, and she'd never felt inclined to use it. But now she needed some breathing room. Or, a voice whispered, are you trying to find a substitute for autumn in Michigan? Irritated, Erin dismissed the idea. She slung her bag over her shoulder and picked up the bouquet on her way out.

A week later Erin glanced hurriedly at her watch as she finished packing all the material she'd need on the trip to Sawyer Air Force Base. Bruce ambled into her office.

"You're running late to catch that flight," he noted.

"I know," she muttered. Snapping the briefcase shut, she moved quickly from behind her desk. "I'll be in touch after I get there," she promised.

He gave her an incisive look. "If I didn't know better, I'd say you were excited about going."

She shrugged, trying to look casual when she was, indeed, brimming over with anticipation. Since spending the previous weekend at Lisa's cabin, she'd been more honest with herself. The two days in the tranquillity of the forest had helped tremendously to restore her torn spirits. She had crunched through the fallen leaves, breathed in the musky smells, and looked for signs of the coming winter. Slowly she had begun to understand why Ty loved the outdoors. She had returned to the office on Monday morning feeling refreshed and clear-minded.

"I'm looking forward to getting back into the woods again," she told Bruce.

"Ah, so you enjoyed the Catskills?"

"It was wonderful," she said, stepping out into the lobby. She turned. "Wish me luck."

"Brother, do I! Think of me when you take that ride in the B-52. I have to admit I'm jealous. But remember our purpose," he added darkly.

On the flight to Michigan, Erin tried to quell her racing heart and relax. The plane landed at Detroit, where she spent several hours waiting for the connection to the small town of Marquette. The weather in New York had been cloudy and threatening rain. Here the sky was a turquoise-blue with a brilliant autumn sun. Glancing at her watch, Erin realized that it was nearly four-thirty and that she was hungry despite her excitement.

The small commuter aircraft landed at Marquette County Airport at exactly six P.M. The sky had turned a dusky apricot and the sun was dipping lower, silhouetting a stand of pine trees against the horizon.

Erin tried to appear calm and collected as she stepped into the main waiting area of the tiny airport. Rapidly she scanned the faces. Ty Phillips wasn't here. Her soaring spirits plummeted, and she wrestled with her disappointment. When had she *ever* felt like this? How could a man she had met and worked with for only two days have such a devastating effect on her a month later? *You've got it bad, Erin,* she chided herself silently. She picked up her suitcase and headed for the front doors, where she peered outside. There was no sign of an Air Force car or any military personnel. Setting down her luggage next to a row of chairs, she dug into her purse for the phone number of the public affairs office at the base.

A frustrating fifteen minutes later, she was still trying to get the PA man on the phone. But he was nowhere to be found, and Security couldn't locate Ty either. With an exasperated sigh, Erin hung up. What next? She would not be allowed on base unless a sponsor signed her aboard, and right now no sponsor was to be found. She was beginning to get angry over the snafu. She walked slowly back to the chairs and sat down, mulling over the situation.

Another ten minutes passed. Looking idly out the glass doors, she noticed a man in an olive-drab flight uniform walking quickly toward the building. Her heart beat strongly. It was Ty! She could tell by his confident walk and proud carriage. She rose, her gaze fixed on his exhausted features, as he pulled open the second set of doors.

She had never before seen an Air Force pilot in flight uniform. Around his neck he wore a rainbow-colored scarf, which was tucked haphazardly beneath the collar of the comfortable-looking one-piece flight suit. An SAC patch decorated the right side of his chest, while squadron and wing patches adorned each shoulder. His name and rank were printed in silver on a black leather rectangle over his left breast pocket.

So many different impressions assaulted her at once. Shadows darkened his eyes and his taut lips conveyed an angry tension. He pulled off his flight cap as he entered and immediately caught sight of her.

He hesitated just an instant before hurrying over to her. Stopping only inches away, so close that she felt his warmth permeating the space between them, he hungrily assessed her upturned face, his appraisal intense and unsettling. "Gal, you are a sight for sore eyes," he muttered fervently, placing his hands on his hips in a characteristic gesture. He broke into a boyish welcoming grin. "How did you grow more beautiful in just a month, Erin Quinlan?"

Her heart leaped at the husky invitation in his voice and all her disappointment vanished. "Is this your way of atoning for being late?" she teased back, meeting his smile with her own. The urge to reach out and be enveloped in his arms was almost overwhelming. He was standing so close, so excruciatingly close. Regarding him more closely, she gave him a questioning look. "Did you just land?"

Ty snorted and picked up her suitcase. "You got it, lady. Come on, I'll fill you in as we drive back to the base."

She fell into the same easy pattern with him once again. He was always a gentleman in every way. He placed her luggage in the trunk of the car and held the door open for her. As Ty slid into the front seat, she said, "Are you sure you aren't a throwback from medieval days? Or are all bomber pilots gallant knights in disguise?"

"Comes with the territory, darlin'. The Air Force Academy pounded into our heads certain rules about manners and protocol. Why? You want me to stop being a gentleman?" He glanced over at her, smiling, and guided the black Pontiac TransAm into traffic.

"Heavens, no! I rather look forward to it, if you want to know the truth," she admitted.

"I always want the truth from you, Erin," he replied more seriously.

She relaxed against the seat, happy to be sharing the same time and space with him once again. "As if an Irishwoman could lie," she baited.

"If you lied, I could see it in your face, darlin'. You couldn't hide a single emotion if you tried."

Suddenly she felt vulnerable under his warming gaze. Had he seen how she really felt about meeting him? Had he sensed her sweet agony at not being able to reach out and touch him? To feel his arms around her once more? She could think of no rejoinder, and so she stared out at the thickly wooded land they drove through. "You looked a little harried when you came to pick me up," she said.

Ty ran long fingers through his dark hair. "I've just finished a sixteen-hour mission, and I really pushed the Buff to get back to base on time." He flashed her a smile. "It was the fastest debriefing I've ever participated in." He laughed. "Those poor guys had writer's cramp before I got through with them." He sobered slightly. "I'm sorry I was late, but my schedule screwed up my flight itinerary. I wasn't supposed to fly today, but we were assigned to be the backup crew in case the other Buff broke down."

Erin widened her eyes. "What do you mean, 'broke down'?"

He shrugged. "You have to remember that these aircraft are twenty-four years old, Erin. The crew aboard S-31 experienced a hydraulic failure before taking off. As a consequence they remained at Sawyer and my crew had to take their intended flight plan instead."

"Does it happen very often?"

"No. Just when I'm supposed to pick up a beautiful woman."

She joined in his laughter. "What now? Do you realize I'm starved?"

"That makes two of us, darlin'. Let me get you installed over at the distinguished visitors' quarters, and and I'll grab a shower at the BOQ. I'll climb back into my uniform and take you over to the officers' club for dinner. How does that sound?"

"But aren't you tired, Ty? You look exhausted."

The worry in her voice did not go unnoticed. He reached out, his hand covering hers for a brief moment. "It's nice to see that you care," he murmured. "Remember, I gave you those two sayings about Buff crews?"

"About being tough?"

"Yup. It's not uncommon to have a sixteen-hour mission, come back, grab some sleep, work the next day for six hours, and then fly the day after on a twelve- or fourteen-hour mission. That's what we mean by *tough*."

Erin drew in a deep breath and shook her head. "My God, why push crews like that, Ty? You can't take that forever, can you?"

"Mmm, depends on your attitude, your crew, and how competitive you are."

"What do you mean?"

"Simply that we fly like this all the time. It's hard, constant work, Erin. We all get fatigued. The only thing that keeps us going is the fact that the crew bands together like a family and supports each other through it. We catch up on sleep when we're out on alert for seven days."

"Alert?"

"Yes. SAC crews have to stand alert ten days out of every month. We're sequestered in a special area with Buffs that are armed and ready to fight a nuclear war, if it ever comes. Which"—he sighed—"nobody wants to happen." He shook his head. "If the alert Klaxon ever goes off, we'll be heading for the Buffs knowing it's the real thing."

"You mean if the alert goes off, that means someone has attacked us?"

"Either that or a dangerous situation has escalated. We're trained to get those Buffs airborne in less than fifteen minutes. We'd be off the ground by the time any nuclear strike hit the U.S."

Erin shivered. "You live in a strange world, Ty," she murmured. "I can't imagine living with that daily. The stress must be terrible."

"Well, maybe now you can begin to appreciate just a little bit when we say, tough enough to fly the Buff. The SAC crews are highly trained, motivated, and intelligent people. But I think you'll see that in the next five days." He shared a smile with her. "I'm upsetting you, I can tell. Let's get onto lighter subjects, shall we?"

"No, I mean—"

"It's all right," he murmured. "Welcome to my world, Erin Quinlan. You're going to find it almost alien at times, frightening at others, and fantastic at still others. You'll find that we play as hard as we work."

A smile curved her lips. "Is that a threat or a promise?"

"Both, darlin'."

Minutes later, Ty ushered her into the distinguished visitors' quarters, which were located a short distance from the officers' club. Erin halted in the foyer of her suite and glanced around. "It's like a very plush home!" she said, turning to Ty as he brought her luggage into the dining area.

He pursed his lips. "This is really something," he agreed. "I've never seen it before." He ambled across the plush carpeted living room, which was tastefully decorated with black leather furniture. "Take a look at this," he said, motioning to a fully stocked liquor cabinet. "If you want to have a party, this is the place to throw it." He laughed.

"I guess," she answered, walking through the living room to a kitchen and four bedrooms. Standing at the entrance to the kitchen, she murmured, "Why don't you go get cleaned up? That will give me time to unpack and get adjusted to this penthouse."

Ty shook his head ruefully as he took one more look around. "Now I know why I have to make colonel. I could get used to a place like this."

"Do colonels and higher-ranking officers have the privilege of staying here?"

"Yes. The rest of us poor Buff drivers stay at either the bachelor officers' quarters or own a home on or off base."

"And you live off base."

He flashed her a smile. "Wouldn't have it any other way."

"Knowing your taste," Erin said, "your home is probably just as richly appointed."

He raised an eyebrow, amusement in his blue eyes. "Oh? How can you tell?"

"When you sent me that lovely bird-of-paradise bouquet, practically everyone who came in to see it commented on how much it must have cost you."

He stood languidly, hands on hips. "I don't care what anyone else thought. What did you think?" he probed.

Erin's lips parted. "I was surprised," she admitted. "No one has ever given me such lovely flowers. I just wish there was some way I could have pressed one of them and kept it forever."

His expression grew more tender as he regarded her in silence. "So, you're an old-fashioned gal at heart," he murmured, as if realizing a new and fascinating part of her. "Pressing flowers and keeping mementos reveals a decidedly romantic streak, you know."

She warmed beneath his gaze. "Just because I don't go around wearing long wool skirts and lace blouses doesn't mean I'm a complete feminist," she challenged.

He raised his hand in farewell. "I like you just the way you are," he reassured her. "I'll be back in about forty-five minutes with the public affairs officer. More than likely he'll want to spend some time explaining the itinerary he's drawn up for you."

"Over dinner?" she hinted.

Ty grinned. "Absolutely."

6

ERIN TRADED HER traveling attire for a blue-gray pantsuit of light wool. She added an ivory raw-silk blouse with a bow at her neck. A touch of burgundy lipstick highlighted her flushed cheeks and sparkling blue eyes. Normally she wore her long hair in a chignon, but she knew Ty liked it loose and free about her shoulders. She ran a brush briskly through the dark strands, which formed a silken frame about her oval face.

A knock on the door interrupted her thoughts. She opened it to find Ty standing there with another officer. She smiled in welcome.

"Come on in," she invited.

"No, let's make introductions on our way to the club," Ty suggested.

She nodded, remembering how hungry he was. "Fair enough." Ty's eyes narrowed briefly, and she blushed beneath his intense inspection.

"Erin Quinlan, meet Lieutenant David Campbell. He's the PA for Sawyer. Dave, meet Erin."

She shook the younger man's hand. He was about twenty-four, with dark hair and brown eyes. "It's a pleasure to meet you, Lieutenant Campbell," she murmured.

He exuded a quiet air of confidence she'd rarely found

in men that young. She wondered if the same was true for most younger SAC officers.

Ty walked at her right side and Lieutenant Campbell on her left as they escorted her to a single-story building half a block away. As her right arm swung freely, Ty inconspicuously caught her fingers for just a moment and gave them a warm squeeze. Erin looked up at him, surprised. He released her hand, but shared an intimate welcoming smile with her. Her heart swelled with joy.

The officers' club had white stucco walls, thick wine-colored carpeting, and a tasteful arrangement of lamps that simulated flickering candlelight along the walls. Ty placed his hand at the small of her back and guided her to the entrace of the dining area. As they paused there, several people looked up. Erin moved closer to Ty, uncomfortable beneath their perusal.

"Hey," one officer in a green flight uniform called to them, "Do you think we oughta let a bomber puke eat here?"

Erin grimaced at the rude name calling, but an irrepressible grin lurked at the corners of Ty's mouth. "Just be thankful we let you tanker toads come here at all," he kidded the officer.

"Hey, who's the good-lookin' woman, Phillips? Did you tell her if you kiss a tanker toad he turns into a handsome prince?"

She blushed fiercely and felt Ty's hand sliding more protectively around her waist.

"That isn't how the story goes, Tom." Ty laughed. "If I remember right, if you kiss a tanker toad, you turn into a frog. Besides, nothing's going to help your face, with or without a kiss."

The men at the table broke into laughter. Ty grinned and glanced down at Erin. "Don't take any offense—

they're always like this," he told her. "Those are the guys who refuel us in the air. They wear red scarves around their necks. Look around here and you'll see some of the guys wearing white ones, or white ones with red bulls on them. That's our way of identifying what outfit they're flying with."

Erin murmured her thanks as he pulled out her chair for her and she sat down, relieved to be less visible to the curious crowd. Glancing over at the PA, she noticed that he appeared to be a bit upset. Maybe distinguished visitors weren't supposed to get the full treatment. She gave him a reassuring smile. Ty was standing near her talking to the tanker crew.

"Are they like this all the time?" Erin asked Dave Campbell.

"Pretty much. It's their way of letting off tension after a grueling mission."

"I know. Ty was telling me that he just came in from one himself."

Lieutenant Campbell grimaced. "I'm sorry no one was there to meet you, Miss Quinlan. That's not our standard policy."

"It's quite all right. It gave me a chance to get a glimpse of Marquette."

"Phillips! Where's that broad we heard was coming on base?" a woman asked, her husky voice carrying halfway across the dining area.

Erin blinked. Lieutenant Campbell frowned. Ty made a half turn, a grin edging his mouth. "Right here, Linda," he said, gesturing toward Erin.

There was a moment of stunned silence as the woman officer stared at her. The woman was clearly embarrassed. Her eyes grew wide, and she gave Ty a disgruntled look, as if blaming him for her blunder. She rose from the table and hurried over to Erin.

"Hi," she greeted her nervously. "I'm Linda and I want you to let me know if these guys don't treat you right. I'm the exec over at the squadron, and I can get them in all kinds of trouble if they misbehave."

Erin smiled warmly, hoping to put Linda at ease. "You'll be the first to know if they don't," she promised.

Linda turned, planting her hands on her hips and glaring up at Ty. "Why didn't you tell me she was here?" she demanded.

He laughed and shrugged. "She was right here all the time, Linda. You could have looked up and seen her come in." He gave the woman an affectionate pat on the shoulder and returned to the table, sitting down. He winked at Erin and chuckled. "She feels terrible. I hope you didn't take any offense at her comment."

Erin had trouble concealing a smile. "No. If she hadn't looked so upset, I would have burst out laughing." She glanced over at a distraught Lieutenant Campbell. "Relax. I haven't had my feelings hurt," she assured him.

After they'd eaten and Lieutenant Campbell had explained Erin's itinerary, Ty escorted her back to her quarters. He held the screen open for her as she unlocked the inner door. She looked over her shoulder at him. "You must be exhausted," she murmured, stepping inside.

He nodded. "I was until I saw you. How about you?"

She shrugged. "I'm not too tired. Why don't you come in? I'd like to discuss some of the details of this itinerary."

His face brightened. "Good. I didn't want to leave yet anyway. We have a lot to catch up on."

Feeling suddenly light-headed, she nodded. "I know what you mean."

Ty made himself comfortable in the living room while

she changed into brown slacks and a pink sweater. When she returned quietly in her bare feet, he raised his head, admiration shining in his eyes.

"Now you look at home," he observed warmly.

Erin felt heat stealing into her face as she sat down on the couch near him, wrapping her legs beneath her. Leaning back against the black leather, she finally felt fully relaxed.

Ty looked incredibly handsome in his dark-blue uniform. It matched his eyes, and Erin enjoyed the feeling of intimacy that ebbed and flowed between them.

He placed the magazine he had been perusing on the coffee table and rested his arms against his long, well-muscled thighs. "I thought Campbell was going to faint from Linda's gaffe." He chuckled. "Did you see him turn chalk-white?"

Erin giggled, putting her hands to her lips. "Yes, and I felt so sorry for her! I thought it was kind of funny."

"So did I, but I couldn't admit it with Campbell there. He does things by the book and probably wouldn't have appreciated the comeback I *wanted* to give Linda. She doesn't know it yet, but she got off lucky this time. Wait until I see her back at the squadron."

Erin joined in his laughter. "You have such a good sense of humor," she observed.

"You need it to take the pressures SAC puts you under, darlin'. We all develop a sense of fun as a necessary release of tension. One of these days I'll tell you about some of the practical jokes we've pulled on each other."

Erin felt relaxed and at home with Ty. Allowing her imagination to run free, she pictured them sitting before a fireplace with glasses of wine. A shiver coursed through her, and she longed to be held in his arms. She stared at his mouth, remembering the only kiss he had given her. Sighing softly, she tucked that lovely memory away.

"You're daydreaming," he interrupted softly, watching her with a curious expression.

She roused herself, caught up in the mood. "I was just wondering why I feel as if I've known you for a long time. After our terrible fight in the airport, and then spending only two days together, I shouldn't feel this comfortable," she mused.

A curious smile played on Ty's mouth, a dark gleam coming to his eyes. "Oh? Why not?" he inquired softly.

Erin didn't resist the temptation to indulge her fantasies and melt beneath his gaze. Alone with Ty, she felt as if the rest of the world had disappeared. All her attention became focused on him alone. She almost forgot she was at an SAC base. The man inches away from her made her feel vital and alive in ways she never had before. Time and space simply ceased to exist for her. She seemed to be magically connected to him in some special way. At these thoughts, her brows drew together in a troubled look.

Ty reached out, his strong fingers caressing her arm. "What's wrong?"

She raised her eyes, meeting his blue gaze. "I feel like I'm home," she whispered, the question "Why?" conveyed in her tone.

He gave her hand a gentle squeeze. "Sometimes, Erin," he said huskily, "we don't know we're going home until we're there."

Her pulse raced. "It's all so crazy..."

"Life is crazy, darlin'. The trick is to learn to flow with it."

"Do you flow with it?" she asked.

"I try to. I'm not always successful, but I give it my best shot."

Erin watched as he entwined her slender fingers with his. A tingle of pleasure raced up her arm. His reassurance steadied her and calmed her inner turmoil. "Ever since you told me about your husband and the hell you went through, Erin, I've done a lot of thinking," he went on huskily.

"About me?" she asked, her voice suddenly hoarse.

He met and held her eyes. "About *us,*" he corrected. A wry smile pulled at his mouth. "I may have worked my tail off this past month, but I still left room for you in my thoughts. Matter of fact, my crew's been ribbing me, claiming I've turned into a daydreamer." He shook his head. "And it's all your fault, darlin'."

Her heart beat faster as she held his gaze. She felt herself opening up to him as easily as a flower responding to the sun's warming rays. "I don't understand..." she began helplessly.

"You must have loved your husband very much to carry the anger you felt toward the Air Force all this time," he said slowly, watching her every expression. "You're a one-man woman, Erin. After he was torn from your side, I think you were left with an emotional void in your life that you're still working to fill."

Erin felt uncomfortable at his probing words and took an unsteady breath. His fingers remained firmly entwined with hers, giving her a sense of security. "You've been doing a lot of thinking," she said softly.

"Darlin', I'm not trying to hurt you." His mouth flattened into a thin line when she remained silent. "Damnit," he swore, "I'm trying to tell you something and it's not coming out right." He pulled her into his arms and tipped her chin up, forcing her to meet his troubled eyes. "Do you know how many times I've dreamed of kissing you again?" he whispered against her cheek.

Erin's lips parted, and she melted into his arms without resistance. "Oh, Ty," she cried softly, straining to meet his descending mouth. A sweet fire uncoiled deep within her as his lips erased the loneliness that had haunted her since she'd left him. He caressed her lips gently, tasting them, lingering sweetly. She slipped her arm around his shoulder and drew his body against hers. He groaned and whispered her name like a reverent prayer. His mouth grew more insistent, parting her lips. She trembled within his embrace as his tongue invaded the depths of her mouth, melting the core of her being. He pressed her into the couch, his hands capturing her face and drawing her inexorably more deeply into him.

She was wildly aware of his lean male body pressing against her pliant curves, of her shallow breathing and his clean masculine scent. His fingers framed her face as he gently kissed her again and again. Her heart hammered without relief as she responded to his strong mouth, wanting, longing to keep touching him.

But finally he drew away, his eyes flecked with the gold of passion. She felt a deep, hungry emptiness that she yearned for him to fill. It weakened her, causing her to tremble. Sensing it, he traced the curve of her jaw with his thumb, a wistful look in his eyes.

"You taste like a fine sweet wine," he murmured, his warm breath fanning her face. He leaned down, caressing her lips once more, imprinting upon them evidence of his need. He drew his fingers through her loose hair. "And such lovely hair," he whispered. "God, how I've dreamed of doing this, Erin," he confessed hoarsely.

She closed her eyes, resting against his shoulder, unable to speak. He had aroused needs she had thought forever dead. No man had ever brought to life the embers of her passion. She felt breathless and stunned. Only his continued touch upon her face gave her a sense of reality. She felt as if she were floating in a heady euphoria, and she couldn't cope with the range of emotions Ty had so easily evoked in her.

"I haven't slept very well since leaving you," he admitted, a hint of wry amusement in his voice. "I lay awake at night remembering your face, your expressions. Erin, do you realize how much you speak with your eyes and lovely mouth?"

She was cradled within his lambent gaze. "No," she admitted, her voice wispy, unsteady.

A tender smile curved his mouth. "When you're happy, your eyes are turquoise with flecks of gold. When you're angry, they're almost black, like thunderclouds on the horizon. Your eyes turn blue-gray when I kiss you." He leaned over, kissing each eyelid. "Like right now. I'd swear they're almost gray." He chuckled softly.

"I never realized—" she began lamely.

He leaned back, gathering her into his arms so that she rested against his broad shoulder. "That's because nobody ever told you before, gal." He gave her a little shake. "That's what you need, you know. To be told how lovely you are inside and out."

His heart beat solidly against her own as she lay with him. Sudden pain mingled with her joy. The anguish deluged her happiness like a storm drenching a sunny day. His coarse light wool uniform rubbed against her cheek. How could she be in the arms of an Air Force officer? One of his kind had killed her husband. And what about the article? Her promotion, her very job, depended on it. She had spent several years preparing to move into a management position. Yet she was here with Ty, an enemy to both her personal life and her professional career. What was happening?

"You wear your heart on your sleeve, Erin Quinlan," he murmured, breaking into her desolate thoughts. "When Linda bulled her way into the conversation and embarrassed you today, you had every right to be angry. But I watched you. I saw you wrestling with surprise and shock." Ty leaned down and placed a kiss on her hair. "And I saw your incredible sensitivity revealed in every change in your expression. You had put yourself in Linda's place. You didn't embarrass her as she did you. Instead, you were gracious and smiling, trying to make her feel at ease so she could gracefully extricate herself from the blunder. That sort of unselfishness is rare, and it makes me want to take you into my arms and protect you from the world."

His whispered words were a balm to her tender heart. She placed a hand on her breast, aware of the increasing pain within her. He was achingly honest and so sincere. When had she ever met a man like Ty? Never.

Shakily she withdrew from his arms and sat up, facing him. Her mouth felt a little sore, well kissed. Ty tilted his head, a questioning look in his eyes. "Talk to me," he urged huskily, making no further attempt to touch her.

She swallowed against a lump forming in her throat, which felt dry and scratchy with unshed tears. "I don't know what's happening, Ty," she breathed. "Not a day went by when I didn't think about you." She smiled wistfully. "Or I'd see contrails up in the sky and wonder if you were flying up there at those high altitudes."

He chuckled. "Probably was. We flew up to Greenland a couple of times. Hey, I see hurt in your eyes. Why?" he coaxed gently.

Tears sprang up, though she tried to stop them. "Uh-oh. Damn, you shouldn't have said that." She sniffed, dashing the first tear from her cheek.

Ty took a white handkerchief from his back pocket and handed it to her. "I'll never understand why you feel embarrassed to cry. What do you gain by holding it in?"

She choked back a sob, half laughing as she blotted at her eyes. "An upset stomach. Ulcers someday, if I don't watch out."

"Crazy, mixed-up woman. What am I going to do with you?" he teased huskily.

In a blinding instant Erin realized she had fallen hopelessly in love with Ty Phillips. More tears filled her eyes, and she fought to stem the rising tide. Ty frowned and muttered something, gripping her arms and pulling her back into his embrace.

"Stubborn woman," he growled. "Now, lie here against me and let those tears fall."

The dam burst and Erin buried her head beneath his chin, sobbing. When during her adult life had she ever been held and cared for? She had always extended her compassion and understanding to others, but she had rarely received what she had needed in times of anguish. Not until now. Ty gently caressed her shoulders and back, his voice soothing, calming.

"That's my gal, let it go. Let it all go. It isn't worth the price of holding it in."

Erin had no concept of time passing. She knew only that Ty was rocking her back and forth in his arms, his chin resting against her hair. At length he loosened his embrace and brushed the last tears from her cheeks. He forced her to sit back on the couch and studied her in silence. "Feel better?" he finally asked.

If he had spoken in any tone other than one of understanding, Erin would have felt foolish. Instead, she dipped her head in answer. "Better," she agreed.

He rose slowly to his feet. "Tell you what I'm going to do, darlin'. I'm going to make you a hot toddy so you'll sleep like a rock tonight. The exhaustion in your face scares me. Have you been putting in long hours?"

She nodded, sniffing. "Always," she muttered. She reached out, touching his hand. "Thanks, Ty..." Her voice trembled with tears. He had such a devastating effect on her. But it was a positive, healing effect.

Ty squeezed her fingers. "First things first. I'll make you that toddy, and then I'll get going. And don't give me that look..."

Her lips parted in wonder. "What?"

Groaning, he walked to the liquor cabinet across the room. "When you look so damn vulnerable and in need of protection, I lose my sense of duty, morality, and obligation," he muttered.

She felt heat stealing into her face when he returned with the drink and was unable to meet his eyes. He stood there, a scowl lingering as he watched her take the first tentative sip. She wrinkled her nose and glanced up at him.

"I'm not much of a drinker," she confessed.

"I know. You like wine instead. But tonight a little Irish whiskey won't hurt you a bit." He looked at his watch and grimaced. "Well, we've both turned into pumpkins. It's after midnight." He gave her a stern look, one that she imagined came very easily when he was dealing with his subordinates. "Drink *all* of that and then get into a hot tub. I'll come by tomorrow morning and pick you up at eight A.M. for breakfast."

She nodded mutely, unable to tear her eyes from his handsome face. He looked so strong and capable. "I owe you," she whispered, meaning it.

Ty pursed his lips. "Believe me, I intend to collect when the time's right, my Irish banshee. Good night." He leaned down, placing a kiss on her hair.

Erin watched him cross the foyer silently. The door opened and closed, leaving her alone in the tranquil silence. The whiskey warmed her insides, and she stared blankly into space. Too much had happened too soon. She had no defense against him or her tumultuous emotions.

7

THE NEXT MORNING Erin glanced out a curtained window and gasped with pleasure at the trees. More than once during the night she had been awakened by the roar of huge jets taking off into the darkness. She was used to her quiet apartment, not to the comings and goings of giant military aircraft a half mile from where she slept. But now the sun was rising against a clear sky, promising a beautiful day. The oak, maple, and tamarack trees had turned many shades of red, orange, and yellow, making the landscape in back of the quarters a veritable palette of fall colors.

Her mood had swung dangerously from one of fear during the night to joy this morning. The memory of Ty kissing her and allowing her to cry on his shoulder sent a mixture of anxiety and longing surging through her. What was happening to her? She was overreacting, not thinking straight at all.

She checked herself in the mirror one last time. Today she had to function as the investigative reporter. She put on a suit of rich chocolate-brown that set off the highlights in her hair. A simple but elegant white blouse with feminine ruffles softened the austere lines of the skirt and jacket. The natural ruddy color of her cheeks and red mouth made her eyes look larger and more alluring. Partly to please herself, and partly to please Ty, she allowed her thick hair to fall around her shoulders.

Ty's face mirrored his appreciation as she stepped outside in response to his knock. "You should have been a model," he murmured, slipping his hand under her elbow and guiding her to the TransAm. The air was warm, and a light breeze playfully lifted Erin's hair, which she pulled back from her face.

"Have you ever considered modeling yourself?" she asked, smiling.

Ty opened the car door for her and waited as she slid onto the seat. "Once a Buff driver, always a Buff driver, darlin'. But thanks for the compliment. It's good for my ego."

As they drove, Ty showed Erin various points of interest. "Over there is C ramp," he said. "That's where we keep all the Buffs that are scheduled for training missions." He pointed over his left shoulder. "And that's the Alert area."

Erin craned her neck, trying to get a glimpse of the highly restricted section. She could see little from this distance except for some camouflage-painted tail sections. "Not much to see," she said, disappointed.

Ty grinned. "Don't worry, you'll get a closer look this afternoon. It's pretty boring for me, but maybe it won't be for you. I see that place once a month whether I want to or not." He commented on a building under construction in which they would eventually hold highly technical simulator training classes to help crews keep their skills sharp when they weren't flying missions. Erin noticed the large number of security vehicles moving slowly along the paved streets, which were crowded with traffic even at this early hour.

"You don't realize you're on a secret installation until you see those guys with guns," she commented.

"The Air Police are nothing to fool around with on this base," he agreed. "They all carry M16's, and they mean business. Wait until you see the security checks we have to go through to get to the Alert Facility. Then it will really sink in."

He took her to a small cafeteria. Erin tried to calm her excitement, part of which came from being with Ty, part from the adventure of simply sharing his world for a few precious days. In line, he scowled and pointed at her tray. "You aren't eating much."

"An orange and some toast will fill me up." She raised an eyebrow. "It looks as though you're eating for two people, Captain Phillips," she observed dryly.

Smiling, Ty paid for their meals and ushered her over to a comfortable booth, where they sat facing each other. Taking off his flight cap, Ty dug hungrily into the food. Erin suppressed a smile. He reminded her of an eager ten-year-old hurrying through his meal so he could go outside and play. Afterward they lingered over their coffee in comfortable silence.

"Around nine we've got to be over at Supply to get a flight suit, helmet, and your parachute equipment," he said. "I should have told you to wear slacks today."

"Why?"

"Fitting a parachute means adjusting the leg straps. I don't think we'll be able to do that, do you?"

She blushed, catching Ty's teasing look. "You're really enjoying this, aren't you?" she accused without rancor.

"Sort of . . ."

"What am I going to do?"

"We'll wait until tomorrow to pick up the chute. Don't worry. But be sure and wear slacks or jeans. I've gotten permission to take you through a Buff tomorrow morning. We'll spend a couple of hours rummaging around inside one. I'll try to explain what we do in lay terms."

"I'd like that," she said sincerely.

Ty raised his chin, catching her widened gaze. "Yeah?"

She nodded. "Of course. I want to understand what makes you tick."

He pursed his mouth. "And that's important to you?"

His softly spoken words created a more intimate mood between them. "Yes, that's important to me," she admitted.

He nodded, slowly turning his coffee mug in his large hands. "What happens, Erin, if you come away from this investigation without the angle your editor wants?" he asked softly.

She frowned thoughtfully. Conflicting emotions assailed her. So Ty had anticipated that possibility too. She spoke carefully. "Bruce knows I would never forsake my professional ethics to write yellow journalism," she said slowly. But deep inside she wondered if even she believed what she was saying. She was reminded of Bruce's accusations—that she was allowing herself to be persuaded by Air Force propaganda, that she wasn't considering all the facts objectively. Her frown deepened.

Worry and concern filled Ty's eyes. "I suspect that the more you learn in the next week, the less an article proposing that we get rid of the bombers is going to make sense to you. But I think you know that already," he added softly. He sighed heavily, pushing away the coffee cup and leaning back against the seat. "I really don't care about the article one way or another, but I wonder if you'll get that promotion if you don't write it the way they want."

Erin was forced to agree. "I don't know either, Ty.

All I do know is that I won't write lies. Not for money and not for a promotion. I can't do that."

"What will happen to your career if you can't write the story they want?"

She gave a helpless shrug. "Oh, I'll be in the dog-house, no doubt."

"And you'd be back on a national beat, traveling more than ever. Something you're trying to cut back on."

"Yes, that's true. I'm not looking forward to sleeping in hotel rooms and running to the nearest fast-food restaurant for another four or five years."

Silence lengthened between them. Erin sensed that Ty was grappling with some problem, but she didn't know what it was. He appeared concerned about her welfare and career, and her heart blossomed toward him with renewed warmth. She leaned forward, her elbows on the table. "Ty," she murmured, "I appreciate your concern."

"I had a chance to do a little investigating on your editor, Bruce Lansbury," he said, surprising her. "We've got a pretty complete library here on the base, and I read a number of articles by him over the past three or four years. He's very opinionated."

She laughed with little humor. "Yes, he's single-minded when he wants to be."

Ty watched her with an indefinable expression in his eyes. "Has he ever railroaded you on any articles you've written in the past?"

"Never. He knows better," she answered firmly. "Bruce and I have an unspoken agreement. Sometimes he does influence a few of the reporters to write things they wouldn't ordinarily put down on their own. I've had arguments, or I should say healthy discussions, with him in the past on what I feel a reporter's responsibilities are."

"What are yours?" he asked.

"To stick to objective facts, not hearsay or emotionalism."

Ty frowned. "A lot of Bruce Lansbury's articles are biased, presenting only one side or injecting subtle editorializing. He tends to stack the deck." He looked over at her. "I don't want you to get the idea that I'm worried about the Triad article you'll write, Erin. What I am concerned about is the confrontation that's bound to occur when your responsibilities as a reporter come up against Lansbury's demands."

"Bruce has always respected my stand in the past," Erin reiterated, unsettled by Ty's warning. She felt he was probing for another specific but unspoken reason. Finally he sat up.

"Your editor is a pretty good chess player," was all he said. "Just be careful, Erin. I don't want to see you get caught in the middle."

She smiled, touched by his concern. "I think you're making too much of it, Ty."

He nodded. "Probably am. Let's talk about something happier—you and me."

Her eyes widened as she studied his face. There was a hint of challenge in his eyes. "Okay, what about you and me?"

"Ready for that picnic tomorrow afternoon?"

"Can't wait."

He tilted his head, his blue eyes dancing with devilry. "Are you sure?" he baited.

"Very sure," she promised. She leaned forward, her hands on the table. "Ty . . ."

He shook his head. "Not now, Erin," he murmured.

She gave him a startled look. "How do you know what I was going to say?"

"Like I said, darlin', everything is broadcast on your face before it comes out of those lovely, inviting lips. And I can't reach out and hold your hands, like I want, because of where we are. I know we've got some serious talking to do." His voice lowered, becoming more intimate. "I'm having one hell of a time keeping my hands off you. A couple of times I just caught myself from throwing my arms around your shoulders and drawing you near me."

Erin trembled inwardly, his voice a delicious caress. "Don't you think I haven't wanted to reach out and touch you too?" she murmured.

He picked up his flight cap from the table. "Tomorrow," he promised huskily. "Tomorrow you aren't going to get away from me, Erin Quinlan."

After taking Erin through the Buff the next morning, Ty drove her directly back to her quarters. He followed her in, smiling. "Quite a plane, isn't she?" he said.

Erin went to the kitchen and washed her hands. They had started at the cockpit and worked their way back through the cramped area where the crew members operated, and her hands were dirty. "I'm impressed," she agreed. "Really impressed."

Ty leaned lazily in the kitchen doorway. "I was impressed too," he responded, becoming serious for a moment. "You enjoyed it, didn't you?"

She dried her hands on a towel and walked past him, hesitating at the bedroom door. "I had a great teacher. What can I say? You made it simple enough so that even I could understand what you guys do." She shook her head. "And I'll tell you something, Ty, I'm in awe of all of you. The amount of knowledge required to fly that huge bomber simply stuns me."

He shrugged, looking embarrassed, then said brightly, "Get changed into some comfortable clothes, darlin'. I want to get off this base to some freedom."

An hour later Erin stepped from the TransAm and looked up at a huge two-story modern house set on a lot heavily wooded with ash, oak, and maple trees. Caught up in Ty's happy mood, she returned his smile as he gripped her hand and led her up the steps.

"So this is how an Air Force captain lives," she drawled. "Must be nice."

He shoved the door open and ushered her into the foyer. "I'm single, remember? I don't have a wife and three or four kids to support. Make yourself comfortable in the living room. It'll only take a minute to change out of this uniform."

Erin wandered into the spacious ivory-carpeted room. A beautifully carved oak mantel framed a brick fireplace. She ran her fingers along the smooth satin finish with appreciation, then gazed around her, noting the blending of creams, peach, and soft gray tones. Dove-gray furniture helped to soften the room. A brass vase contained graceful sugarcane stalks, providing a personal touch.

"Who did your decorating?" Erin called, standing on her toes and glancing down the hall to the right.

Ty ambled out of the bedroom dressed in well-worn jeans, in the middle of shrugging into a short-sleeved blue shirt. His broad chest was covered with a mat of dark hair, and his muscles flowed, attesting to his peak physical condition. He began to button the shirt as he headed for the kitchen. "Does it matter who decorated it?" he asked.

Erin followed him, making herself at home on one of the two bamboo stools at the counter. "Yes."

He began to take several items out of the refrigerator and place them on the counter before her. "Why?"

She sighed with exasperation. "Do you know, you can be very irritating when you want to be, Ty Phillips."

He laughed and pulled a wicker basket from a cabinet. "I love to tease you. Your eyes get wide and even more beautiful, and you get a petulant set to your lips." He reached over, brushing her hair back across her shoulder. "Don't pout too often, darlin'. You'll get wrinkles—or kissed," he whispered, setting the basket before her.

Her heart leaped in response to his brief silken touch. She was momentarily irritated when she felt the heat of a blush stealing into her cheeks. Until she'd met him, she'd never blushed! "You're infuriating," she said, trying to maintain a grave tone.

He gave her a wicked look, his blue eyes dancing with mischief. "Why should it make a difference if I decorated this house or someone else did?"

"Because, you stubborn Irishman, if you did, it tells me something about you," she answered, losing her patience.

"Well, I did, so what does that tell you, Miss Quinlan? That as a kid I was good with crayons?"

She stifled a laugh, watching him neatly place food and utensils in the basket, including a chilled bottle of rosé wine. "You're crazy," she accused.

"All Buff crews are, believe me," he responded fervently. He lifted the basket and, coming around the counter, gripped her hand. "Let's go. I'm starved and we've got a two-mile hike before we get to a real special place. Ready?"

Erin smiled up at him. "Ready."

He led her out the back door and down the wooden steps. The ground was covered with freshly fallen leaves.

Ty seemed to know exactly where he was going, without any hint of a trail. A warming breeze moved with them as they wound more deeply into a grove of trees. Leaves twirled and spiraled down around them. Erin inhaled their sweet scent.

"This is lovely," she said softly, breathing in deeply.

Instantly Ty's hand tightened about her fingers. "Not half as lovely as you are," he murmured.

She looked up in surprise, caught off guard by the depth of feeling in his voice. "Stop it," she whispered, slowing her pace.

Ty frowned down at her and pulled her to a halt. He set the basket beside them and took a firm hold of her shoulders. "Why?" he demanded huskily.

Erin stared helplessly up into his face. "Don't you realize that this is only a dream?" she said painfully. Feeling miserable, she tore her gaze from him. "I feel so..." She groped for the right word.

"Frightened?" he provided, placing his hand beneath her chin and forcing her to meet his gaze.

"Yes," she admitted. "Scared, frightened, afraid to reach out for something I need desperately. To me, this is like a dream come true, Ty," she confessed, the words tumbling out. "It's a stolen moment in both our lives, something unexpected that came up out of nowhere. You take my breath away every time I think of you," she whispered. "And I realize that each minute, each hour I spend with you, is like my own lifeblood to me. I was starving and didn't know it, not until you came into my life. You were supposed to be an adversary. Instead—" She choked back a cry, trying to pull out of his grip.

"Erin," he commanded gently, giving her a small shake, "why do you see this time together as stolen moments? You act as if this is some sort of magical interlude. Once you leave, it's over. Is that what you're saying?"

A myriad of emotions clashed violently within her as she stared up into his clear blue eyes. Oh Lord, he was so strong, so capable of giving her the balance she needed in her life.

Ty released her slowly and slid his arm around her waist, drawing her next to his body. He picked up the basket and they continued to walk at a slower pace.

"Keep talking to me, Erin," he commanded. "I never got the impression that you wanted a brief fling."

"Do you think—"

"Now, take it easy! Don't get that Irish temper of yours up. When I met you, I knew you weren't the type for a casual affair. You play for keeps, just like I do." He leaned down, kissing her hair. "From the very first, you entered my heart, Erin. I don't let many people get that close to me, but you did. It was as if I didn't have control over myself anymore. At first it scared me, just like it scared you. No woman has ever intoxicated me like you have. Believe me," he said, catching her startled gaze, "we were both deeply affected by one another. I purposely left you alone for that month to think about it—about me and maybe about us." His voice took on a more hopeful tone. "No one was looking forward to your coming up here more than me, darlin'. No one."

His admission sent a thrill of joy through her. She gave in to the euphoria and leaned her head against his broad shoulder. "No one except me," she corrected.

As if Ty sensed her need to consider his admission, they walked the rest of the two miles in companionable silence. His arm around her waist was reassuring, and she was grateful for his care. He always seemed to know when she needed to be held. And wasn't that a part of love? A current of shock went through her. She loved him. The thought made her even more fearful of the future.

Finally Ty drew her to a halt at the edge of the woods. Before them stretched a brilliant-green meadow, a bright contrast to the orange, yellow, and red of the surrounding trees. A gasp of delight broke from Erin's lips as she regarded the tranquil scene. "It's beautiful!" she exclaimed.

Ty gave her an enigmatic smile. "Come on, you can help spread the blanket," he urged. Within minutes Erin sat cross-legged on the smooth blanket next to Ty, unwrapping sandwiches while he uncorked the wine. A pair of squawking, raucous blue jays flew overhead.

"Reminds you of a pair of jet fighters taking off," he said.

"They're certainly noisy enough," she agreed, passing him a roast beef sandwich.

He poured wine into crystal glasses. She admired the steadiness of his hands and asked, "Do you have the same firm touch with the Buff?"

He grinned. "Nothing to it." He pointed to his well-developed forearms. "See this? I didn't get these from lifting weights, believe me. They come from jockeying that aircraft around for refueling, which can be very difficult at times."

"And we'll be doing a midair refueling tomorrow?"

Ty nodded, sipping the wine. "We do one on every mission, just to keep in practice. Fighters do it too, but they remain hooked up to the boom extension from the tanker for about thirty seconds. We're on the line for fifteen minutes or so. And when you're riding around on bumpy air, you come out of it feeling like a wet dishrag."

"It doesn't sound like very much fun," she agreed.

"You'll be there to see and experience it all," he promised genially. Then he became more serious. "You're in a pretty lucky position. None of the wives can fly in a Buff. Sometimes they can hop a ride on a tanker and watch their husband's Buff being refueled, but that's it. I'm glad you have the opportunity to really understand the pressures the men are under."

She gave him a searching look, trying to figure out why he had mentioned that. Giving up, she ate hungrily and drank her wine. Afterward they relaxed on the blanket. The wine had made Erin feel languid and happy, as if nothing could go wrong in the world. Ty cleared away the remains of their meal and set the basket off the blanket. He lay on his side, facing her. A warm breeze moved through the meadow, kicking up stray leaves here and there. He reached out, grazing her temple, his fingers sliding through her hair.

"You look more relaxed," he observed, allowing his hand to rest on her upper arm.

She gave him a rueful smile. "It's the wine," she confessed. "I feel a little high."

His warm expression tore at her senses. "I'm high on you, Erin Quinlan," he whispered, caressing her cheek gently.

She shivered pleasurably at the touch of his fingers and sought out his gaze. "Ty, where are we going?" she asked breathlessly.

Outlining her brow, he murmured, "I'm not sure. But I want the chance to find out with you."

Her pulse beat strongly at the base of her throat. He slid his hand beneath her neck, bringing her gently off balance and pressing her back against the blanket. He lingered above her, smiling reassuringly. Each stroke of his hand soothed away her fears of an unknown tomorrow. He rose to a sitting position and placed his arm across her so she couldn't escape. Not that she had any desire to leave.

Leaning over, he sought her mouth with his. He pressed gently, parting her lips, coaxing her to return the desire he conveyed. She tasted the bittersweet wine on his mouth and a soft moan rose from her throat as she moved against his strong, powerful body. The brush of his rough cheek against her own and his appealing masculine scent dizzied her awakened senses.

He broke away from her then, barely brushed her wet full lips, teasing her, demanding her response. She sighed raggedly, her heart thundering in her ears, an aching, fiery hunger spreading throughout her body as he moved his hand slowly up her long torso, following the curve of her breast. Mindlessly she traced the lines of his shoulders, her fingers curving into his soft hair, pulling him down to her.

His mouth molded firmly against her waiting lips, hungrily taking her, his tongue stroking her inner depths. He provoked wild shock waves of desire, and she arched against his hard body. She was losing control, becoming like malleable clay within his masterful hands. She was vaguely aware of his fingers expertly unbuttoning her blouse, the material slipping away, exposing her taut, expectant breasts. He seemed deliberately to torture her by removing her lacy bra with excruciating slowness. Her fingers dug convulsively into his shoulders as he dragged his mouth from hers, finding and teasing her hardening nipples. A sharp moan of pleasure rose from her lips as he aroused her to near-frenzy. She felt wanton, untamed, and yearned to be ever closer to him.

It was as if time had slowed to a halt. She lay cradled

within a spiraling vortex of need. Each touch, sight, sound, and smell was amplified to a throbbing degree. She felt the hot sun beating down on her naked body, felt Ty's own masculine unclothed body against hers. Running her fingers across his broad chest, she gloried in the mat of dark hair beneath her exploring hands. She heard him groan as he pulled her possessively beneath him. The burning ache intensified, and she moved her hips upward. His fingers wrapping tightly in her long tangled hair, he forced her back against the blanket, sliding his other hand beneath her hips. Her breath came in ragged gasps as she arched to meet him, whispering his name, begging him to fulfill their union.

An explosion of white fire shattered her remaining hold on reality. An incredible surge of pleasure coursed through her, hot molten liquid melting her core, and she sighed, tears bathing her cheeks. Ty murmured her name over and over against her ear, his hot breath fanning across her face.

He claimed her lips hungrily, bringing her into rhythm with his body. Heady with an intense, thrilling pleasure, she responded to his coaxing. And then, suddenly, all her aching yearnings became focused in a moment of intense desire, and she was released to soaring ecstasy. A cry of joy broke from her lips, and she pressed tensely against him, the ultimate gift of love shared between them. She floated mindlessly in a euphoria within his arms, vaguely aware that he groaned, and gripped her convulsively against him. A tremulous smile touched her lips as he rolled onto his side, taking her with him.

She lay in Ty's protective embrace, the warm sun on her body, the breeze caressing her damp skin. She snuggled closer to him, tracing the curve of his cheek and jaw, not wanting to relinquish contact in any way. He stroked her hair, placing small kisses on her eyes, nose, and finally her throbbing lips. Their hearts thundered in unison, a joyful reminder of what they had just shared.

After some time, Ty rose on one elbow, his eyes still simmering with passion as he caressed her with his gaze. He gently lifted a curling tendril from her cheek and, smiling tenderly, leaned down, parting her trembling lips with a lingering kiss.

Erin rested her hand against his chest in a gesture that returned the love conveyed in his achingly sweet kiss. He cupped her face, his eyes dark with adoration. "My beautiful banshee witch," he whispered thickly. "How loving you are..." He slid his arm around her, holding her tightly for a long, reverent moment.

"Ty," she whispered brokenly, "hold me, just hold me." She felt as if a new world had been laid at her feet, and she couldn't bear to part from it just yet.

A long time later, they slowly dressed each other, trading caresses, tender kisses, and intimate gazes. Erin finished buttoning Ty's shirt and gazed up into his eyes. In that blinding instant she knew she never wanted to leave his side. As if sensing her surrender, he leaned over and brushed her parted waiting lips with his. She felt she might explode from utter happiness. Might she die from such jubilation? She snuggled back into the crook of Ty's arm, where he held her close.

The sun rested just above the forest of pine and oak, its long rays slanting across the meadow and striking the hillside where they remained in each other's arms. They seemed to be captured in a magic spell as they savored the hour with solemn attention given to each other.

Ty rested his head against Erin's cap of silken hair. "I don't ever want this day to end," he murmured.

"Never," she agreed, closing her eyes and nuzzling his chest with her cheek.

"I was right," he said gently. "You are a banshee witch. You cast a powerful spell, Erin. I've never experienced anything like this in all my life. Not ever . . ."

She reached up, caressing his face. "It was as if we had always known each other, as if we were simply reestablishing some lost, forgotten tie from the past."

He nodded, embracing her tightly.

8

THE MISSION BRIEFING began at eight A.M. the next morning at the 644th Bombardment Squadron headquarters. Erin had little time to remember the day before, a day that had changed her life. She wondered if it had changed Ty's life, too.

He escorted her through swinging doors into the headquarters. Most of the SAC crewmen were wearing light-blue shirts and dark-blue serge slacks, while a few others wore the familiar green one-piece flight uniform. Erin flushed furiously beneath the stares of the curious men. She walked with Ty toward a row of cubicles to their right, each of which contained a table and eight chairs. She was grateful for Ty's hand at the small of her back as he guided her toward the first cubicle.

"Hey, here's our SAC trained killer!" a large chunky man greeted them.

"You're just jealous, Guns," Ty returned. He pulled Erin to a halt. "Men, I'd like you to meet the lady who's going to be flying with us tomorrow. Erin, I want you to meet the best stand-board crew on base."

She noted that they all grinned at one another with pride. Ty introduced his crew individually, beginning with a young man of about twenty-six to her right.

"This is the co, short for copilot, Barry Rhodes. What you see him doing with all those figures and that calculator is distributing our fuel load on the Buff. He makes sure that the various fuel cells located all over the wings and fuselage are evenly utilized. That way the Buff doesn't get lopsided, and we don't end up with a weight distribution problem. He's my right-hand man on every flight. Couldn't do without him. Barry, meet Erin."

Barry Rhodes rose to his full six feet and extended his hand. He had a kind face and light-blue eyes. Erin smiled as she shook his long sensitive-looking hand. It struck her that the men who actually flew the Buffs had hands like artists'. Maybe it took a special creative artistry to fly the huge bomber.

"And this is the guy whose shoulders ought to be broken by the responsibility he carries. This is our radar bombardier, affectionately called 'Radar' when we're on a mission. John Nedzelski is responsible for making our crew number one for electronically scored bomb runs in the squadron."

John got up, a broad smile creasing his almost gaunt face. He appeared older than the others, his medium-brown hair thinning at the front and top. He pushed silver-framed glasses up on his nose. "A pleasure, Miss Quinlan. And don't listen to Ty. He's only telling you part of the story. If it wasn't for some fancy flying by the AC here, I wouldn't have a score to tally up."

Erin gave Ty a questioning look. "AC?"

"Sorry," Ty said. "Aircraft commander. That's my title when something goes wrong and they need somebody to haul in and chew out. You'll hear me called 'Pilot' or 'AC' during the flight. "This good-looking lieutenant is our navigator, Ray Owens. We call him

'Nav' on the flight. He keeps us on course and gets us home safely."

Ray blushed, a broad smile lighting his rounded, slightly squirrel-cheeked features. "Don't let them fool you, Erin. They call me and John 'mushrooms.'"

She laughed with the rest of them. "Mushrooms?"

"Yeah," the chunky man at the end of the table said good-naturedly. "Tell her why."

Ray turned the brightest red Erin had ever seen and glanced up at Ty, who chuckled.

"Go ahead," he urged. "She's a tough lady. She can take a joke."

It was Erin's turn to blush. She shot Ty a murderous glance. He sent a wicked look in return, seeming to enjoy the moment immensely.

"Well," Ray began, "we sit down on the lower deck of the Buff. The other four crewmen sit up in the daylight and can see the sky. John and I are in a small compartment with little elbow room and it's really dark. For the entire flight we've got the red glow of the navigator and bombing instruments, plus each other. That's it. We never see sunlight until we step off the Buff at the end of a mission."

"Ah," the co teased. "Tell her why you two are called mushrooms. You're sidestepping the point."

John, who seemed a bit more sedate and mature, spoke up. "Erin, do you know how mushrooms are grown?"

"Well—" she began, searching her memory.

"They're covered with manure and put in the dark to grow," he explained dryly.

The entire crew broke into hearty laughter, and Erin felt her face grow red.

"Yeah," Guns added. "You notice both of them are balding? They're the only two."

"Gee." The co chuckled. "You guys must be close to reaching maturity."

Ray wrinkled his nose. "Drop dead, Co."

Erin couldn't suppress a giggle. Ty was right; he had a crazy crew. But their camaraderie was heartwarming. They made her feel accepted and she began to relax beneath their teasing banter.

Then Ty introduced her to a tall, lean man at least five years younger than Erin. "This guy is our EWO, or electronics warfare officer, Skip Helman. He's responsible for jamming the enemy's signals and keeping SAM missiles away from the Buff. Skip's a very special breed of SAC and without him none of us would survive."

Helman had a quiet, intense air. He gravely inclined his head as he shook her hand. She was struck by the heavy weight of responsibility he'd assumed at an early age. The same was true of many of the others. Their youthfulness seemed inconsistent with their image. At last Ty led her to the jovial man at the end of the table. "This turkey is our gunner, Andy Welsh. We always call him 'Guns.' He's the only enlisted man in the all-officer crew, and he's responsible for keeping fighters or other offensive weapons off our tail."

Ty invited Erin to sit down at his left. "How are you guys coming with the planning?" he asked.

"Another three hours and we ought to have most of it," the co said, frowning as he punched more numbers on the calculator.

Soon they all settled down to business. Ty explained that they would be flying a William Tell mission, which meant that the bomber was to act as a decoy target for fighters off the Gulf Coast of Florida. "Fighter pilots have to stay proficient at hitting moving targets, so they try to score a hit electronically against the Buffs," he said, showing her their intended flight path on a map. "We'll make two low-level passes at three hundred feet just off the coast."

"They won't nail us," Guns said confidently, breaking into a grin.

The co snorted softly. "They may not hit us, but they'll claim a score anyway. Look at this, Ty," he muttered, shoving a form under his nose. "All we get is a forty-five-degree bank in either direction in a very limited air corridor. It'll be hard *not* to hit us," he complained.

Erin glanced at the orders and then up at Ty "What does he mean?"

"In training exercises like this, where we're acting as decoys, we're not allowed to use the full range of evasive action we would under actual war conditions. If one of these fighters was five miles away, hunting us down with heat-seeking missiles, I'd have that aircraft doing some radical maneuvers to throw the fighter off our track. But in this exercise, we're more or less stable targets for the fighters."

"Sitting ducks," Ray corrected, frowning. "We're making it too easy for those fighter jocks," he complained.

"Hell"—Guns chuckled—"what do you expect of the fighter pilots? They've all had frontal lobotomies. We can't expect them to hit a moving target, can we?"

The men broke into a collective snicker. Erin gave Ty a questioning look. "Do you hate fighter pilots?" she asked.

"No," he answered innocently, trying not to smile.

"You ever met any, Erin?" Guns asked.

"No."

"Good. You aren't missing a thing, then," Ray added.

Ty grew serious. "There's always been a strong good-natured rivalry between the fighter jocks and bomber crews," he explained. "They think they're pretty good, but so do we."

"Do they think you're slow or something?" Erin asked, not quite grasping the source of the rivalry. "You fly a much larger, heavier aircraft."

Guns chortled again. "Say, she's bright. You're close, Erin. Those jocks have got egos a mile wide. They get all the glory, all the press for heroics. Meanwhile, while they're buzzing around like gnats in the sky, we're bringing along the heavy thunder. We can do more damage than any one of them."

She sat back. "Sort of like the tortoise-and-the-hare fable, eh?" The crew nodded.

Erin rested against the door of her quarters. It was nearly ten P.M., and she felt pleasantly weary. Ty placed his hand against the frame near her head. A sympathetic smile hovered around his mouth as he gazed down at her.

"You're tired. But it looks like you enjoyed yourself today."

"I did. I loved every minute of it." She sighed. "And I love your crew. What a great bunch of guys. Now I'm beginning to understand what you mean by your 'other family.' You all support and care for one another in many ways."

He grinned. "Yeah, they're all crazy as hell, but that's what it takes to be in this field and stay sane."

"SAC trained killers," she murmured, shaking her head. "The image you guys have with the public, and what you really are—they're as different as night and day."

He leaned closer. "Which do you prefer?" he asked huskily.

Erin craved his closeness. They had been together all day but always conscious of the need to maintain a proper distance. At times the urge to reach out and touch him had been almost unbearable. How often had she stared into his strong face, remembering the branding imprint of his mouth on her own? Now she inhaled his male scent and closed her eyes. "I prefer the man who made love with me yesterday," she whispered. She raised her lashes, meeting his dark gaze. She longed to slip her hand into his, to lean against his solid length.

Her face must have broadcast her wishful thinking, for Ty's eyes shone with an understanding glint. "Sometimes, darlin', it's better not to think of the past," he murmured. After touching her cheek in a light caress, he straightened up. "Better get to bed," he said. "We've got a busy day ahead of us tomorrow."

She sighed deeply and opened the door reluctantly. "You're right. Good night, Ty."

He stood there for a long moment before turning away. She felt as if an invisible magnet were pulling them together. The excruciating urge to take one step forward and fall into his arms was almost overwhelming. She had seen the same desire in his turbulent gaze. He wanted her as much as she wanted him.

But, no, it wouldn't be right. Not while each of them had professional responsibilities to fulfill. Turning, she walked into her quarters and closed the door behind her.

Erin felt awkward in the green flight uniform. Dutifully she tucked the rainbow-colored scarf around her neck and folded the ends across her chest, just as Ty had instructed her. She shrugged into the matching green jacket and picked up her camara case. The rain hammering at the window suited her morose mood.

Just then a knock sounded and she clomped through the living room, finding the required black combat boots very awkward.

When she opened the door, Ty looked her up and down, pleasure dancing in his eyes. He looked freshly showered and clean-shaven, his dark hair still damp. "Gal, you're a knockout. You sure give a flight suit new meaning," he teased, smiling broadly. "Ready?"

The sight of him lifted her spirits. She slipped out the door. It was dark: wind and rain slashed at her face. They dashed to the car and slipped inside, dripping water on the seat. Ty slammed his door shut, muttering, and ran his fingers down his thighs. Abruptly he turned and gripped her shoulders.

"Come here," he whispered huskily, his breath warm against her cheek. "I wanted to do this all day yesterday." He pulled her forward, his mouth pressing against her lips, parting them, tasting them with hungry urgency.

She moaned softly and relaxed against his chest, curving her arms around his neck. His mouth was warm and enticing, a pleasurable shock to her responding body. The faint smell of soap mingled with the masculine scent of his skin. She returned his kiss as he spread his fingers through her loose hair. Then he gently pulled her away and stared at her with unconcealed passion.

"You had that coming," he said, his voice thick.

Her breathing was shallow and erratic, like her heartbeat. He took her breath away. He'd stolen her heart and he held it captive in his strong and gentle care. "Tell me what I did to provoke that, and I'll do it again," she teased.

But he ignored her invitation. Although he allowed

his hands to slip from her shoulders, he continued to hold her gently for a long time. His expression grew serious. "I've got some bad news, Erin," he finally said.

Her euphoria vanished in an instant. She frowned, concerned. "What's wrong?" Her throat felt tight and the words came out squeaky and high-pitched.

He squeezed her hand firmly. "Eight hours after I finish this damn flight today, my crew has to go on alert."

She gave him a confused look. "I don't understand."

"It means, beautiful lady, that our time together is almost over," he whispered huskily.

Her stomach twisted into a hard knot. Pain curled through her, and an ache began in her throat. She swallowed convulsively, tearing her gaze from his anxious face, staring blindly out the rain-streaked window.

"Look," he began hoarsely, "it wasn't originally planned this way. But there's been a schedule change. The squadron leader contacted me late last night. Lieutenant Campbell will escort you around the base tomorrow." He sighed heavily. "I'm sorry, darlin'. I didn't want it to end this way."

She turned slowly back to him. "End?" Her voice wobbled. "Is that all this relationship means to you?"

His face hardened, his eyes grew darker. "No, damn it. Lord, don't look at me that way, Erin! It's enough to tear my guts out."

She dashed away a tear. "I'm sorry," she apologized thickly.

He reached over and gripped her shoulders. At first she resisted. "Don't fight me," he warned. "Come here. Come here and let me hold you."

She capitulated. Falling into the safety of his arms, she rested her head on his broad shoulder. He kissed her hair. "This isn't the end," he growled softly. "We met and crashed into one another, Erin. From the first moment I saw you, it was as if I had known you forever. Two days...for just two lousy days we were thrown together at Wright-Patterson. I felt torn apart by the month-long separation that followed. We've been able to re-establish something very special in the last several days." He embraced her tightly. "Beautiful, unforgettable days, Erin. We need the time, darlin', and we just aren't getting it. Somehow we've got to find time to get to know one another better, and under less pressured circumstances."

Erin pushed herself into a sitting position, her hair in tangled disarray around her face. She met his concerned eyes, her heart constricted with pain. "I want the time, Ty," she admitted. "It all happened so fast. It wasn't supposed to...I mean..." She groped for words to describe indescribable feelings. Releasing a shuddering sigh, she added, "I'm afraid, Ty. So afraid."

He caressed her cheek. "Why afraid?" he asked gently. "We need time, that's all. There's nothing to be afraid of, darlin'."

"But don't you see?" she cried, her voice strained. "The article."

"What about it?"

She sniffed and, accepting the handkerchief he offered, dabbed her eyes. "At first I was ready to write a blistering commentary on SAC and why we should get rid of the bombers. But as I got to know you, talk with you, I saw the other side of the story. The more facts I gathered, the more convinced I became that I couldn't write against the bombers. And then, Ty, these last few days. These men and their families put up with so much to defend our country. I'd feel like a traitor if I capitulated to Bruce's demands and wrote something I didn't believe in."

Ty held her. He spoke in soothing hushed tones and stroked her hair. "Erin, you have to separate feelings from facts, you know that. You're a damn good reporter. If the facts don't back up what your editor wants, then don't write the article."

She raised her head and stared at him. "I got a phone call last night too," she admitted, her voice barely audible. "From Bruce."

"And?"

She twisted the handkerchief in her fingers. "He wasn't at all happy with my analysis of the situation."

"Facts are facts," Ty reiterated. "What does he want if the facts don't fit the story he's after?"

"He—accused me..." She shut her eyes tightly. "Oh, damn, I did it to myself," she whispered.

"You're not making sense," Ty growled. "What did he accuse you of, Erin?"

She gestured helplessly. "At first it was all business. Then Bruce said he noticed that every time I mentioned your name, my voice changed. He asked if you meant something more to me than just an escort. I couldn't lie," she admitted, "so he accused me of being persuaded by a decoy to write a different article on SAC."

"Damn him!" Ty's eyes blazed. "You know that isn't true, Erin."

She held the handkerchief against her lips. "I know! But he's prepared to write an article accusing me of being brainwashed if I don't take the slant he wants!"

Ty gave her a guarded look. "Blackmail?" he demanded, his voice a dangerous whisper. "He's blackmailing you into writing it or he'll mention your name in print?"

"Mine? I don't care about mine!" she cried. "It's your

name, Ty! Now that I know how important your career is to you, I can't jeopardize it. An article on *me* would embarrass you and all of SAC. I can't risk that."

He leaned against the seat and stared angrily out at the rain. His mouth became a thin hard line, but he remained silent. Finally he turned to her and said, "What do you want to do? How can I help?"

Her heart opened with love for him. He wasn't going to abandon her! She felt a new protectiveness toward him; she wanted to shield him from public embarrassment. "Nothing, Ty," she whispered faintly. "This is something I have to do on my own."

"No, it isn't, damn it!"

She jerked her chin up, startled by his outburst. He gripped her hand. "That's part of your problem," he said earnestly. "You're so used to surviving by yourself that you've forgotten how to work as part of a team. Well, this issue involves *both* of us. Even if I didn't care for you the way I do, I'd still try and help you solve it. What he's trying to do is wrong."

Her lower lip trembled. "He's got me boxed in on all sides, Ty."

"I could alert SAC headquarters to his tactics. Maybe I could wangle some leave to fly to New York and meet him on his own turf."

In that moment Erin loved him fully. She could no longer deny what she had felt for him all along. He was proving himself to her as no one ever had before. He was willing to risk his career to protect her.

"No," she whispered. "Just let me handle it in my own way. Maybe, just maybe, I can convince him to change his mind."

Ty gave her a skeptical look and released her hand

reluctantly. He glanced at his watch. "We've got to get over to the squadron, Erin. We won't have a chance to talk about this during the mission. After debriefing I'll have a few minutes alone with you. Maybe then we can come up with a satisfactory answer to this dilemma."

9

ERIN GRATEFULLY DRANK a cup of hot coffee as Ty picked up the crew members and drove them slowly through the wind and rain to C ramp. The gloomy weather lowered Erin's spirits still further as she stared out the fogged-up window to see great gusts of rain flung into distorted shapes by heavy winds. Guns sat in the seat behind her and supplied her with information about the base and the Buff they would soon be flying. He seemed the most lighthearted member of the crew; the others were unusually quiet and serious.

Finally the bus pulled to a halt in front of one of several Buffs painted in camouflage. Everyone scurried toward the dropped hatch door beneath the belly of the bomber.

"Go on up, Erin," Guns shouted into the wind.

Soaking wet from the brief jog to the plane, she climbed shakily up a narrow ladder. After clambering onto the metal grating of the lower deck, she hesitated. It was dark, and a chilling cold invaded her body. Groping blindly, she found the rung of the second ladder, which led up into the small, cramped cabin area. Bending over, she walked to the bunk, which was located on the port side of the Buff, and sat down, trying to stay out of the way of the crewmen, who were boarding.

During the next five minutes gear of various sizes and shapes was lifted up the ladders. Erin helped Guns stuff bags containing helmets and oxygen masks on the bunk. Other equipment was stowed in odd nooks and crannies between huge panels of instruments, which were located on either side of the narrow passageway leading to the cockpit. The light was dim within the main cabin area, and everyone's breath formed moist white clouds, giving the interior an alien atmosphere. Finally the co climbed aboard, took the right seat, and switched on the heat.

Ty was the last person to board, after having made a final check of the outer surfaces of the aircraft. He was soaked. His face glistened and water dripped from his jaw and chin as he edged past Erin. He turned his head slightly, as if to make sure she was all right. She noticed that his eyes looked different; they seemed to hold a new intensity.

She felt a subtle unspoken excitement building within the cabin. An indefinable but palpable sensation throbbed throughout the plane, as if a slow drumbeat were increasing in tempo. Each man knew his job. Each shouted directions and cracked jokes. Erin returned to the bunk and waited until Guns had stowed away the last box lunch.

"Okay, let's get you checked out," he said, rising.

The instructor pilot's seat, called the IP seat, was located directly behind the pilot's. There was just enough room to wedge it between the two other positions. Erin's knees would be within inches of the throttles at Ty's right.

Guns crawled forward and gave the sturdy metal chair a sideways yank. It slid into the center of the deck on a set of specially designed skids so that it was directly behind the throttles between the pilot's and copilot's seats. He motioned for her to sit down.

Erin made herself comfortable on the metal seat, while Guns checked out her parachute, which doubled as a cushion for her back. She struggled into the shoulder harness and adjusted the straps around her thighs. Satisfied, Guns gave her a thumbs up, meaning everything was okay. She was sitting on her pack, which consisted of a radio, survival items, and a small inflatable life raft. It also acted as a cushion, and it was attached to her chute so that, if she had to jump, the pack would automatically come too.

Guns then showed her the seat belt and shoulder straps to be used in heavy turbulence during the flight. "On takeoff, landing, and during low-level runs you have to wear the helmet and gloves, and be completely strapped into your chute and seat belt," he told her.

She nodded. "I understand."

"Great. Now, let's get you hooked up to the intercom so you can hear all the dirty jokes these guys are trading back and forth." She put on lightweight earphones with large mufflike cushions. Guns showed her where the radio jack was located and switched it to the "on" position. "If you want to talk to someone, switch to 'private.' That way everybody else can go about their business and they won't be listening in on your conversations." He showed her several other channels, including those that allowed aircraft-to-aircraft or intercabin communication. Another channel broadcast hard rock music. Guns grinned. "Hey, all the comforts of home." He laughed. "We can even pick up radio stations while we're flying at high altitudes. Kinda takes the edge off the boredom when things are quiet," he explained.

Erin shook her head, feeling as if she had stepped into a whole new world. She understood even better than before what Ty meant when he said the crew was a substitute family to the men. Her spirits lifted simply because she was sharing a part of their world.

She watched Ty working through a thick book along with the co. They were going through a standard preflight check list. She was struck by his expression of intense concentration.

The number of instruments in front of her was mind-boggling. The entire console was a myriad of gauges and dials. Of special interest to her were the small televisionlike screens in front of each pilot's seat. She watched as Ty turned one on. As it warmed up, a picture congealed, showing the ramp in front of the B-52. Erin was dumbfounded. They actually had a camera that could see beyond the small cockpit windows that embraced them on three sides.

For an hour the crew went through the mandatory preflight checklist. Then Erin sensed mounting excitement as the ground crew outside started each of the eight jet engines on the bomber. The plane shivered like a live creature as each of the seventeen-thousand-pound-thrust engines caught and roared to life. A buffeting wind slammed against the aircraft as it sat out on the ramp, adding to the vibration. Finally all eight engines were operating, and Erin replaced her headset with her helmet.

Ty glanced at her briefly. It seemed he missed nothing as his eyes covered her from helmet to feet. "Don't forget your Nomex gloves," he warned her.

She nodded, fumbling for the button that had to be pressed in order for him to hear her. "I won't. Thanks."

He gave her a thumbs-up sign and went back to work. The radio chatter between the ground crew, the individual stations in the Buff, and the tower became intense just before they rolled forward. The bomber trundled heavily off the ramp, heading for an area known as the "hammerhead." Once they were on the warm-up ramp, which lay directly off the runway, Ty would run up each engine to verify its maximum working order. A vehicle called "foxtrot" would circle the plane, making one last visual inspection of the wing and tail surfaces before the bomber actually took off. The weather had turned ugly, and Erin could see that the rain had reduced visibility.

"Pilot to IP. Ready for takeoff?"

Erin jerked her head up, startled by Ty's voice. She was the IP! Fumbling for the button, she stammered, "Ready!"

"Get that oxygen mask strapped on," he commanded.

She snapped the mask across her face and rested her hands tensely in her lap as Ty guided the huge bomber off the hammerhead, aiming the nose down a long strip of runway. Setting the brakes, his fingers closed gently over the eight throttles and worked them forward to the thrust gate. The bomber engines rose with a new high-pitched whine and the entire aircraft shivered. After making several last-minute checks with the tower, the co gave Ty a thumbs-up signal.

He released the brakes, and the bomber crept forward. Erin had expected to be slammed back in her seat from the thrust. Instead, the plane slowly gathered speed, the growling of the engines deepening as Ty kept his hand on the throttles. The aircraft shuddered each time it hit a depression or bump on the runway. The gray landscape became a blur.

"Seventy knots," he said. "Ready, ready—now!"

"Twenty seconds," Nav returned quickly. There was a pregnant pause, tension strung as tight as a taut wire.

"Committed," Ty called, placing both gloved hands on the yoke. The co immediately placed his hands against the throttles, making sure they remained against the thrust gate.

The bomber hurtled down the runway, gathering speed. "Coming up on unstick," Co announced tensely. "Ready, ready—now!"

Ty pulled back on the yoke. Immediately the jolting sensations ceased, and she realized with an incredible surge of excitement that they were airborne. The Buff nosed up into the thick, swirling clouds.

Soon they broke through the last layer of clouds into a brilliant blue sky. Guns, who had been sitting in a sling-type seat just behind the IP, crawled around the corner and tapped her arm. "You can take the helmet off now."

Removing the helmet was like getting rid of an impending headache. She placed it on the bunk and gladly put on the lightweight earphones, hooking back into the intercom. For the next fifteen minutes everyone relaxed. Ty turned, giving her a brief warming smile.

"What do you think so far?"

Her pulse raced at the intimate glance he shared with her. "It's breathtaking."

He winked. "You look like a kid at Christmas."

Soon they flew out over the Great Lakes, where they were met by a KC-135 refueling tanker. Once again Erin had to put on the helmet, mask, and gloves. Her breath caught in her throat as she watched Ty deftly maneuver the huge bomber to within thirty feet of the tanker, which flew just above them. The tail boom from the tanker contained a large retractable hose with a nozzle on the end. Erin's heart pounded as Ty inched the bomber closer and closer until they were flying directly beneath the tanker. His left hand gripped the flying yoke, his right hand constantly monitoring the throttles as he urged the Buff the last few feet. She saw the pipe extending beyond the upper windows and then heard a distinct *clunk*.

"Contact!" the co called, relief in his voice.

"Now we're taking on fuel," Guns informed her. "Actually, we don't need it, but in order to keep the pilot's skills up to standard, we have to refuel on all training missions. Ty will be flying like this for about fifteen minutes."

Erin looked at Guns in awe. "It seems like such delicate work!"

"It is. There's only about thirty feet between us and the tanker. That isn't much when you consider the size of these aircraft." He grinned. "You ought to be here when the weather's rough. Man, whoever's flying comes out of it looking wrecked. The plane has a refueling autopilot," he said, pointing, "but there's a lot of physical strength involved in keeping the Buff between that twelve- to sixteen-foot extension on that boom." He pointed at Ty. "Watch him," he said. "You'll see what I mean."

To Erin, Ty looked like an alien from the very foreign world of combat. Wearing the olive-green camouflage helmet, with the dark visor drawn down across his eyes and the oxygen mask strapped on his face, he was unrecognizable. He was a combat pilot, all business. She heard his clipped tone and watched the sensitive monitoring of his fingers, which rested over all eight throttles. His left hand gripped the yoke solidly, and she watched as he gently coaxed the bomber over each small air pocket. They flew an invisible oval-shaped track above the lakes. Erin's awe increased as the tanker and bomber banked in unison to the left, the bomber maintaining contact with the boom. She shook her head in amazement at the skill these men displayed.

"Pilot to IP," came Ty's voice. "We'll show you an emergency release. We'd use this maneuver if there was the chance of an air accident. Hang on."

Erin held her breath. Ty pushed the yoke forward and the Buff dropped like a rock. Her stomach rose in her throat as it dived three thousand feet in mere seconds. When Ty leveled off the Buff, Erin saw the tanker above her retracting the boom. She shook her head as Ty glanced over his shoulder. He pushed up his dark visor and unsnapped the oxygen mask from one side of his face. His smile made her feel warm inside. "Well? What did you think of that?"

"It made me feel queasy." She laughed. "But excited. It was fantastic!"

"Wait till you get down to low level," the co warned. "We're anticipating thunderstorms in the area. Might get a little turbulence."

"Not to worry, you guys," Guns piped up, coming around to Erin's right. He opened a bottle and dropped two tablets in her hand. "Dramamine. Take them now so you can enjoy the low level."

Soon a new mood pervaded the cabin. Erin enjoyed the view as they leveled off at thirty-nine thousand feet. She was aware that Guns was busy behind her, but she didn't pay much attention. For the next ten minutes she watched and listened to Ty and Barry discussing their intended route. Then she smelled something burning! She pressed her intercom button, a note of panic in her voice.

"What's burning!"

"My cookies!" Guns yelled, jumping up from his cramped position.

Erin unstrapped herself and twisted around. Guns jerked open a small oven across the bunk and slid out a tray of chocolate chip cookies. The distinct odor of burned cookies wafted through the cabin.

"For God's sake, Guns, the least you could do is watch them so we could all have some decent cookies to eat," the EWO chided.

Erin had never laughed so hard. Guns mournfully dumped the burned cookies into a garbage bag. He distributed the edible few among the crew. Ty tapped her knee to get her attention. "We don't want to give you the idea we work hard all the time." He grinned broadly, devilry returning to his eyes. The co was flying now, and Ty was able to give her his undivided attention. "With a long mission like this, we usually have maybe a half hour or an hour before we start working."

"Hard," Radar added fervently.

Ty nodded. "You'll see."

Erin couldn't suppress a laugh. "I didn't know you had an oven in here. It's almost like home!"

Ty agreed and some of the tenseness left his face. "Everything but the kitchen sink. Guns is our chef on board. He brought along a roll of chocolate chip cookie dough and he's probably got his Fritos—"

"Which everybody steals," Co interjected.

"Yeah, mushrooms like them a lot," Nav piped in, hinting.

Erin traded broad smiles with Ty, loving the feeling of closeness among the crew. Guns crawled forward and sat back on his heels as he offered them less burned cookies from his second batch.

"The problem with this little oven," he complained, "is that it only has one temperature, so you have to watch 'em real close."

"Or they burn," Nav teased. "Where are my Fritos?"

"You mushrooms are really noisy today," Guns observed. "Of course, it isn't every day we get a good lookin' lady aboard, either."

Erin felt a blush staining her cheeks. All too soon the banter ended. The Buff quickly covered the north-to-south expanse of the United States. Ty ordered her to strap in with full gear because they would soon be going low level to act as decoys out in the Gulf. Out the cockpit window she could see the blue ocean coming into view. She strapped into the IP seat and tensed as the intercom talk picked up between Nav, Radar, and the pilots.

The Buff had been flying at high altitude, but it descended quickly under Ty's guidance. By the time they hit the marshlands ten miles inland from the Gulf, they were skimming along at fifteen hundred feet. Radiant heat from the sun poured into the cabin, making everyone uncomfortably warm. The Buff jounced and trembled as it encountered air pockets. Sweat began to trickle down Erin's body. She dropped the dark-green visor over her eyes to keep out the blinding sunlight and watched in silent fascination as the video screens in front of them showed not only the elevation of the land they were skimming over, but also a clear picture of the terrain ahead.

Suddenly Erin felt transported into another realm, another dimension. She felt as if they were in a genuine combat situation. The men spoke in clipped voices, and the Buff bucked as it left the coast of Florida, heading over the sea leg of the journey. Ty took the bomber down to one thousand feet and flew a large triangular pattern. Suddenly Guns shouted, "I see him! Five miles out off our tail."

Ty wrenched the yoke to the left, and the Buff sluggishly heeded his order. They banked, the ocean coming closer. He brought the Buff back on an even keel for only a moment before banking again, this time to starboard. The co held the air map in his lap, calling off coordinates. The intercom became jammed with calls, orders, and commands. Ty nosed the Buff down as they roared over the sandy coast, aiming for the marshes. They were now skimming along at five hundred feet. Erin could see every shanty, every wire on the electrical transmission towers, and every bird that was startled out of its nest as they roared overhead. The heat in the cabin rose even higher, and she felt as if she were on the verge of suffocating.

"They got us," Co said.

"No!" Guns returned sharply. "No way! I had that bogey four miles out."

"They're saying they nailed us," Co repeated.

"Those turkeys have been known to lie, too," he shot back, irritated.

"Don't worry, Guns," Ty soothed, his voice grim. "Next time we'll know what to expect and give them a run for their money. Everybody hang on to their stations."

Erin's heart beat in unison with the throbbing jet engines as Ty brought the Buff around in a wide circle, heading back toward the Gulf. There was a heightened tension palpable in the Buff, a current that lived and breathed through each crewman. The pilots talked in clipped tones, their voices filled with new determination.

The second time Ty tested the limits of what he could do with the B-52 to avoid being hit. The fighters lay about five miles off the coast trying to electronically score missile hits. This time the Buff flew away without a single hit being scored against it.

"I think we just thumbed our nose at them," Radar drawled.

Erin laughed as the entire crew broke into a cheer. The co gave Ty a thumbs-up signal, as if to say, "Well done."

"So much for the fighter jocks thinking we're easy targets," Co chortled.

"We did well," the pilot commended everyone. "Let's get back to work. We've got more low-level flying to do."

Erin raised her brows. "More?" she asked, surprised.

"We don't just hang around in the sky for ten hours wasting gas," Ty told her. "We'll be doing several more bombing runs, both high and low, before we return to Sawyer. Sit back and relax, darlin'."

10

From the Gulf they headed northeast across Georgia. At a prearranged coordinate, Ty banked the Buff to the left toward Tennessee. When they had obtained high altitude once again, the entire crew seemed to give a collective sigh of relief. Guns busily heated coffee, which he had carried aboard in a five-gallon dispenser. Erin unstrapped herself and distributed the coffee to the pilots, then to the men on the lower deck.

Ray gave her a broad grin and a thumbs up when she arrived at the lower deck. He and John were wearing their helmets. Erin pressed the intercom button. "Is this why both you guys have thinning hair?"

John grinned. "Because we wear these helmets all the time?"

She nodded. "Don't they get awfully heavy?"

"Nah," came the EWO's voice over the intercom. "It keeps their swelled heads in line."

The entire crew broke into snickers over the intercom and Ray turned red. Erin couldn't help laughing too. She noticed that it was quite a bit rougher down on this deck. "Don't you get sick down here? It's so dark and cramped. How do you take it?"

"Easy," Guns replied merrily on the intercom. "Mushrooms love it!"

"Stuff it, Guns," Nav returned.

"Watch it. I got another batch of chocolate chip cookies comin' up. Hey, I even got a frozen macaroni and cheese dinner. Anyone want to trade their box lunch for it?"

The intercom was silent. Erin glanced at Ray. "Where did he get a frozen macaroni dinner?"

"From home. Often when we're flying long missions we bring TV Dinners aboard and cook them in the convection oven."

"With my help as chef," Guns reminded them tartly.

Ray hit the intercom. "Yeah. Your dainty little fingers just burned the hell out of the cookies. Need we say more about why there aren't going to be any takers on that macaroni dinner?"

"Stuff it, Nav," Guns retorted crisply.

Again the Buff encountered a few rough up-and-down drafts, and Erin gripped the ladder and braced herself against the bolted chair by the radar. "How on earth does the Buff take this kind of beating?" she asked.

Guns was the first to answer. "Look at it this way, Erin. We take them up and do our best to tear them apart. Then we give them back to the Operational Maintenance Squadron, or OMS, to repair."

"Yeah," the EWO added. "The real force behind us is the ground crews. They can repair ninety percent of the problems on a Buff right at Sawyer, which is really something. We've got eleven hundred people working on the ground to keep us in the air."

"And we've got the best OMS around," Ty added. "I once saw a hole the size of a gallon milk jug torn in a Buff's main wing spar. Maintenance cut out the section and riveted another piece of metal in its place. They're something else."

"Hey, Erin," the co spoke up, "do you know that engine number eight was replaced a few hours before we took off?"

Her heart gave a thump of surprise and sudden anxiety. "They replaced an *engine?*" she asked meekly.

Ty laughed. "Don't be frightened. It's done all the time. Part of OMS's job is to take oil samples from each of the eight engines after every mission. They run the oil through a spectrum analyzer to test for metals or other foreign substances. In the case of engine eight, a large accumulation of titanium registered, which meant a bearing was going. So they took out the engine and put in a replacement."

"That's impressive," Erin murmured. She was beginning to understand the tremendous effort it took to keep the SAC bombers in the air.

"The colonel we have at Maintenance is the best in SAC," Ty said. "His people love him, and they usually end up working six days a week. They work five days for the Air Force and the sixth for him. He inspires that kind of loyalty."

"We try our damnedest to wreck 'em and he fixes 'em," Guns added. "What can we say, Erin? We've got the best for the best!"

She gave Guns a perplexed look. "I don't see you trying to tear them up."

"As I've said, the Buffs are thirty-one years old," Ty told her. "These missions put a lot of strain on them. They're such old planes that often something does break or go wrong."

She looked at him quizzically. "But that's dangerous."

"Exactly. We all try our best to keep the Buff safe to

fly, but we need the B-1 B bomber as a replacement, if for nothing else at least so that it won't fall apart in the air."

Erin considered his comments. No other bomber in history had served so long in the front lines of defense for the U.S. The Buff was an old plane in many ways, and she could understand the crew's concern about its airworthiness.

The chatter diminished as Ty brought the heavy bomber to a higher altitude after the last low-level run. Erin climbed back up to the main cabin and strapped into the IP seat.

She heard another radio transmission and she pressed the headset against her ears, trying to pick up the nearly unintelligible jargon. Not succeeding, she watched the pilots. The co's face immediately showed disappointment. Ty twisted around. "You hear that?"

She shook her head. "No. What's wrong?"

"That was Sawyer. There's a blizzard in full swing back at the base. With three-quarters-of-a-mile visibility, a three-hundred-foot ceiling, and winds of forty to fifty knots." He grimaced. "We aren't going home. They're ordering us to divert to a southern base. Keep your ears open. You might pick up some interesting talk." He turned and asked the co to pull out maps showing various air bases in the South.

There was a lot of grumbling among the crew. After a long flight, they wanted to go home to their families. The co looked the most disappointed. Guns chortled over the intercom. "Hey, let's make Barksdale. Man, I love that Louisiana area. Hey, Erin! I know more people down there. We could party all night!"

She turned and grinned. "The way I'm feeling right now, all I want is a hot bath and bed."

Guns shook his head. "Aw, you're just like the rest of these turkeys—homebodies and party poopers."

Erin listened intently. The pilots discussed the amount of fuel they had left and just how far they could fly without the situation becoming critical. Ty finally decided to land at Blytheville Air Force Base in Arkansas, which brought a groan of protest from Guns.

"Man, that's out in the sticks! Know what we call it, Erin? Hooterville! Oh, well." He sighed. "I know a great little place off base where we can get the best barbecued pork sandwiches in the world."

Erin shook her head, smiling indulgently at his enthusiasm.

"Maybe after we finish mission planning tomorrow, we'll commandeer a truck and drive over there for lunch. How about it, Ty?"

"We'll see," he said, busy up in the cockpit.

The sudden need to divert threw the navigator and pilots into a flurry of intense activity. Getting new headings and weather briefings, and alerting the new air base that they were literally dropping in on them, created heavy radio traffic for the next fifteen minutes. Finally the cabin quieted down.

"Ty, where will we stay?" Erin asked.

"Probably the bachelor officers' quarters, unless it's filled up. If it is, we'll get a motel off base."

"And we'll fly back tomorrow morning?"

He shrugged. "I don't know. I'll have to call Sawyer after we land to find out what's up." He gave her a worried look. "Knowing SAC, I bet they'll put us on a night mission on the way back to Sawyer tomorrow."

She gasped. "But you just flew today! Don't you get a rest?"

"SAC doesn't believe in letting us fly a straight line

back to our base, even if we get diverted because of
weather. They'll give us the night to rest up, and we'll
start planning for a night flight tomorrow morning. On
our way home we'll probably take in a six- or eight-hour
mission."

Her frustration and disbelief must have shown in her
eyes because Ty gave her an understanding smile. "I told
you we worked hard. Now you're going to get a taste of
the real thing."

In contrast to K. I. Sawyer, where a blizzard raged,
Blytheville was a quiet air base near the Tennessee border.

The crew disembarked without incident. All the equipment that had been stowed aboard had to be removed as
well. Erin pitched in and helped ferry it to the waiting
bus. It was dark, but the temperature was in the low
sixties, and she found her flight suit bulky and uncomfortable in the warm weather.

She followed the crew to the debriefing room in another building and received stares from several men as
she sat down next to Ty. The debriefing was mercifully
quick. Then they ambled over to the BOQ, only to find
that it was filled to capacity. Thanks to Guns's resource-
fulness, they were able to commandeer a van. Soon they
were heading for a motel five miles away.

After checking in, they met in the adjoining restaurant,
where they drew stares from civilians, since they had
brought no clothes and were forced to wear their green
flight suits. Ty pulled out a chair and motioned for Erin
to sit down next to him. He traded brief smiles with her
as he pulled the flight cap off and stuffed it into a zippered
pocket.

Erin realized she was famished, and everyone else's
order reflected the same degree of hunger.

Afterward, over coffee and dessert, the talk centered on her. The co leaned over, his elbows on the table. "Erin, did Ty ever tell you about the B-52 statistics?"

She gave him a wary look, detecting a hint of laughter in his voice. "No. Is this some kind of joke?"

The crew laughed. Nav blushed furiously. "Nah. Not a joke, Go ahead, Co, tell her."

Erin glanced at Ty, who maintained a poker face. She knew she was being set up now. "Okay," she said bravely, "tell me."

Co grinned broadly, his blue eyes dancing with humor. "There are three facts and a conclusion, Erin. First, the Buff has enough aluminum and steel in it to make twenty thousand garbage cans."

Her eyes widened. "Twenty-thousand!"

He held up his hand. "Second, the Buff contains so much wire and cable that if you laid it end to end, it would stretch a hundred thousand miles."

"That's incredible!"

Co nodded sagely. "Third, with eight engines, the Buff has the power of twelve thousand locomotives." He paused dramatically. "So, we can say the following about the Buff—it flies like twelve thousand locomotives pulling twenty thousand garbage cans on the end of a hundred thousand miles of wire!"

Everyone at the table rocked with laughter. Imagining the ludicrous picture, Erin joined in. "You're the last person in this crew I'd expect to pull a joke like that!" she finally told Co.

Guns hooted. "Don't trust any of us, Erin. We're all crazier than hell!"

Just then Ty excused himself, returning a moment later with an amused expression and a walnut plaque in his hands. Erin gave him a confused look.

"Ordinarily anyone who flies in a Buff gets a paper certificate to acknowledge the achievement," he told her. He glanced at his men. "We didn't want you to forget us so easily. You've been special to the flight and we've all enjoyed having you." He pointed to the date. "Guess you'll have to somehow scratch in another date, since this is turning into a two-day flight."

Erin was deeply moved as she took the plaque. She glanced at the men, a soft smile playing at the corners of her mouth. "Thanks," she whispered. "It's been special for me, too."

"Read it," Co urged.

The blue metal had been engraved with silver to depict a B-52 flying between clouds. Beneath it was her name and the following: "You've gotta be tough to fly the heavies!" It marked the date of the flight, the designation of the mission, and the names of all the crewmembers. She felt close to tears. "It's beautiful," she managed, looking at all of them. "Believe me, I'll never forget this flight, or any of you."

"Or the burned chocolate chip cookies," Guns added.

The EWO gave Guns a friendly jab in the ribs. "Yeah, you really singed your tail feathers on that one, turkey."

Later the group broke up to go to their motel rooms. Ty walked Erin down the hall. She held the plaque against her breast as she slowly drew to a halt in front of her door. Ty looked so handsome, despite the dark shadows under his eyes. "You're really tired," she noted with concern.

He leaned against the wall and gave her a lazy smile, folding his arms across his chest. "Comes with the territory, darlin'. I just want you to know that everyone thinks you've been a real trouper on this flight. Some of the crew were taking bets that you'd end up like a lot of other passengers."

She tilted her head, enjoying his closeness, the feeling of intimacy created whenever they were together. "And what happened to them?"

He grinned. "They ended up sleeping a lot. Most of them couldn't take the hundred-percent oxygen and the fact that the cabin is pressurized for only eight thousand to ten thousand feet. Above that, your blood gets only eighty percent of the oxygen it needs, and you become tired quickly." He reached out, capturing a lock of hair and placing it behind her ear. His light touch sent a small shiver of pleasure through her. "You must have a good blood count," he surmised.

"No." She laughed softly. "It's that stubborn Irish stock we both come from."

"Probably." He turned serious. "You know, you almost had to take a commercial flight home tonight."

"Why?" She was stunned. The thought of leaving Ty and the crew upset her.

"Talk on the subject went up to Eighth Air Force and back down again."

"What are you saying?"

He roused himself, standing up straight. "Civilians are never allowed on night missions, which is what we're flying tomorrow."

"I don't understand," she said, confused.

"They're dangerous, darlin'. We're flying at three hundred knots five hundred feet above rough terrain. We file our flight plan with the FAA, as does a lot of other air traffic. The problem comes from private aircraft, which don't have to file a flight plan with the FAA. We come roaring in low level over sparsely populated areas, mostly

the desert or mountain regions, hoping we don't run into
one of those private planes. Someone at Eighth Air Force
okayed your going along. You do have the luck of the
Irish."

Erin stared up at him in shock. "My God! You mean
those civilian pilots won't know we're there?"

He smiled wryly. "We don't know they're there either,
darlin'." He caressed her cheek, a wistful look in his
eyes. "You're going to be working tomorrow," he promised. "Whoever sits in the IP scans left to right for planes.
It's all visual. The co and I are going to be damned busy,
and we can use your help. If you spot a dark shape, don't
waste time getting on the intercom and telling me to
climb. If you happen to spot flashing lights, just tell me
where you see them and keep a check on them."

Erin exhaled a shaky breath. He was serious. "These
training missions...you fly them all the time? It's so
dangerous."

Ty laughed softly. "It's tiring, fatiguing, and sometimes dangerous. We've had a few near-misses with civilian aircraft, but don't worry about it. You'd be surprised
what can be done with a Buff if there's a potential for
collision."

"I'll make very sure I'm strapped in tomorrow," Erin
promised gravely.

Ty moved closer, his hand cupping her chin. "Even
in a flight suit you look beautiful," he whispered, his
breath warm against her face. "I've had a hell of a time
keeping my hands off you today." His mouth descended,
pressing, parting her lips. His fingers tightened against
her neck, pulling her into his arms. She trembled, de-
siring his strong mouth, his firm, knowing touch. The
contact with his body was pleasant and heady as she

rested against him. He kissed her hungrily, and she returned his ardor. Reluctantly he drew away, his eyes dark with barely checked passion. "I'll see you tomorrow morning," he murmured huskily. "And stop looking at me like that or I won't be held accountable," he growled, a wry smile quirking one corner of his mouth.

It was almost eleven-thirty the next night when they landed back at K. I. Sawyer. Signs of the recent blizzard were everywhere, but the runway was clear of snow and ice. Erin rode on the ramp bus back to the squadron with the crew.

The night mission had been grueling. They had dropped down into the narrow valleys of the Smoky Mountains, making low-level-penetration bomb runs, which were scored electronically by a station below. The flight had started at three in the afternoon and, as dusk arrived, they had dropped from high altitude to five hundred feet, roaring over the heavily wooded terrain. Erin had grown accustomed to the intercom chatter and was able to sort most of it out. Strapped into the IP seat, she had begun to watch for dark shapes in the clouds. Afterward Ty touched her knee with his gloved hand. "You did a good job," he assured her.

She forced a tired smile. "Let's see—I spotted two stars and one plane. Not bad for an amateur."

"Not bad at all," he said sincerely. "We always like someone in that IP seat, if we have an extra body aboard. Everyone is grateful you had the mettle to do the job and do it right."

She had been exhausted by the tension and concentration required. But her job had been easy compared to what the crew had to do. Scanning their faces, she detected signs of their fatigue. Yet there was that familiar togetherness, that teasing humor that bonded them even now.

Ty sat next to her in the bus, his hand draped casually over the seat near her shoulder. He offered her a small smile, which she returned. All too soon he would be gone. The thought sent her high spirits plunging.

After debriefing, Ty drove her back over to the distinguished visitors' quarters. The stormy weather had passed, leaving the base cold and the wind cutting. Erin was glad to enter the warm quarters and take off her oversized boots. Ty lingered in the living room, watching her in comfortable silence.

Dark shadows ringed his eyes and his face looked somewhat gaunt, perhaps because he hadn't shaved in over twelve hours. She put the boots aside and gazed over at him from her seat on the couch. He looked dizzyingly handsome in his flight suit with the rainbow-colored scarf at his throat, the flight cap dangling from his fingers. His dark hair was still damp with sweat. He pushed away from the door and walked slowly over to her.

"You all right?" he asked, his voice dropping to a husky whisper.

Looking up at him, she felt her heart wrench with pain as she realized just how much she would miss him when he left on alert. "I'm fine," she said softly.

He knelt in front of her, resting his hands on her thighs. "I'm proud of you. You took the mission like a real pro. We've flown reporters before, but none of them have done as well as you did." His eyes held a glimmer of admiration in their depths. "But then," he whispered, "you're made out of the right stuff."

Wearily Erin rested her head against his broad shoulder. Did he ever get tired? Good Lord, she felt as if she were made of jelly. He slid his hand over her back, and she warmed to his touch. They held each other for several minutes before Erin pulled away.

"I don't know if I'm made out of the right stuff or not," she admitted softly. "Going back to New York and trying to work a compromise with Bruce on this article is going to be the biggest battle of my entire career."

Ty caressed her cheek. "If I could, I'd be there," he said, his eyes darkening with unspoken affection. "But if I try to get leave now, they'll have to put my whole crew on leave."

She shook her head. "The crew does everything as a unit, doesn't it?"

"Most things. Do this much, Erin. Call me. Keep me informed." He cupped her face, imprisoning it, his eyes intent. "I'm going to see you again, and sooner than you think. We deserve the time to get to know each other better. You're special, lady. So damn special." He pulled her gently to her feet, his arms capturing her body against his long length. "Any objections?" he asked, nuzzling his cheek against her hair.

Erin leaned heavily against him, sliding her arms around his shoulders. "Hold me, Ty," she begged.

He groaned and tightened his embrace. "Forever, if you want," he muttered thickly. Raising her chin, he traced the outline of her lips with his thumb. Her parted lips hungrily met his descending mouth. He molded her body against him, making her fully aware of his desire for her alone. A sweet warmth uncoiled deep within from her as she drank deeply of his plundering mouth, never wanting the kiss to end. She quivered beneath his insistent hands as he awakened her body to new heights of awareness.

At last, reluctantly, he released her, his eyes a turbulent blue. She shivered within his arms, feeling his need for her, wishing that time were on their side, wanting to fall back into his arms and be loved thoroughly. He groaned softly and kissed her lips tenderly. "When I first met you, I thought your eyes were your most beautiful feature," he whispered against her ear. "I was wrong. It's your sweet, full lips." He kissed her again, this time more demandingly. "This isn't the end, Erin," he promised huskily. "We've had a rough start, but that doesn't mean we'll stop trying." He ran his fingers through her silken hair. "Tell me what you're feeling," he coaxed.

She shivered deliciously, feeling like a cat being stroked. All she wanted was to surrender mindlessly to his ministrations. "I don't want you to leave," she whispered. "I feel cheated, Ty. I'm frustrated by your schedule and by my own." She gazed at his strong features, thinking again how handsome he was, despite his fatigue. "I want to be with you when the Air Force doesn't have control over you."

An understanding smile pulled at his mouth. "I'll work on it," he promised, caressing her cheek. "We'll have time, honey. Getting mixed up with a bomber pilot means cultivating some patience." His smile deepened. "And I know a banshee witch doesn't have much of that commodity."

Erin felt buoyed by his affectionate teasing. "You're worth developing some patience over, believe me," she whispered against his mouth.

11

ERIN STARED MOROSELY out her office window, watching the drizzle of a gray November afternoon. Had it really been ten days since she'd left Ty? Her brow wrinkling, she turned halfheartedly and stared down at the rough draft of her article on SAC. She rubbed her face tiredly and gazed longingly over at the telephone.

Ty had called every day from the base. His voice had helped her immeasurably to get through the miserable days without him.

Bruce, her editor, had remained aloof and watchful since her return. He was gruffer than usual. He hadn't changed his mind about the slant of the article one iota. She didn't even want to remember the explosive argument they'd had just yesterday.

Just then the phone rang.

"How's my beautiful banshee witch today?"

She sighed with longing. "Oh, Ty . . ."

"You sound worried."

She closed her eyes briefly. "The same old thing—I'm caught between a rock and a hard place."

Ty's voice lost its teasing tone. "You can't sit on that powder keg forever, Erin. You have to either write it or tell him no."

"I know, I know. Right now I wish I could go up to that cabin in the Catskills and just escape."

"Your friend's place?"

"That's right. I find myself wishing for two things everyday—your call and being at the cabin."

He laughed gently. "It's nice to be number one on your list, darlin'."

"You've been number one ever since I met you," she said, a smile curving her lips. "And you know it."

He joined in her laughter. "This place isn't the same without you. My crew is pining away for you just like I am."

"You always say the right thing to make me feel better," she told him softly, wishing he were here, holding her in his protective embrace.

"Not always," he hedged. "That's why I called a little earlier than usual today, Erin."

Her spirits plummeted, and she gripped the phone tightly. "What now?"

"Our crew is being ordered out on a secret mission for nearly a month. I can't tell you where I'm going or why. And I won't be able to contact you except maybe with a letter or two. I'm sorry. I don't like this any more than you do."

It was the worst kind of news. She had relied on his daily call. It provided at least some connection. How many times had she wanted to tell him of her love? She frowned, moistening her lips, fighting down her anguish.

"The only good thing is that we'll be back by November twenty-ninth."

"You don't even get Thanksgiving off?"

Ty laughed. "Darlin', the military doesn't recognize holidays. Listen," he urged, growing serious once again, "I want you to keep the week of December first through the seventh open. Our crew is getting leave then, and I want to come and see you. We have some important things to discuss, Erin. How about it?"

She looked glumly at the calendar. The dates seemed so far away! "Of course I'd love to see you," she answered, her voice tremulous.

"I'm glad, honey," he soothed. "Just know you're in my thoughts, Erin. And in my heart. You've never left there. Not ever."

Erin's secretary, Ruth, glanced worriedly at her. Ruth had just completed typing the final manuscript on the SAC article. It was the day before Thanksgiving, and everyone in the office was in a festive mood except Erin. "What do you think?" she asked her secretary.

Ruth grimaced. "I think you're putting your head on the chopping block. This isn't a compromise article at all. Bruce has been in such a foul mood lately, Erin. Why don't you just let this go the way he wants?"

Erin tightened her lips and began cleaning out her top desk drawer, throwing several items into the wastebasket. "I'm tired of sitting on the fence, Ruth. Thanks for your concern, but I want you to take that article in to Bruce. Please?"

Her secretary gave her one last distraught look and left the room. Erin collapsed at her desk, staring moodily down at the sheaf of reports she had collected on the SAC Triad. It didn't matter anymore, she thought grimly. Taking a deep breath, she glanced anxiously at the open door. It was ten A.M. and she knew that within an hour Bruce would be buzzing her on the phone and asking her to step into his office. She found herself wondering how Ty would handle a similar situation.

Frowning, she played idly with a paper clip. Would

she be as calm, cool, and efficient as Ty had been when his job had required it of him? He worked seventy hours a week and got home maybe ten days out of the month. He believed in what he was doing and was willing to make the necessary sacrifices. She found his dedication inspiring now. To stand up for what she believed in, she was willing to sacrifice her promotion, even her job.

Bruce Lansbury called a half hour later. Oddly, she was almost relieved that the moment of truth had finally come. Memories of her flight in the Buff flashed across her mind as she walked determinedly across the hall to the editor's office. There were many forms of combat, and she was ready to fight.

"You wanted to see me?" she asked as she walked into Bruce's plush office.

He raised his head, displeasure evident in his expression. He motioned brusquely for her to sit down. Erin complied, trying to appear at ease despite the icy tension between them. Bruce tapped his pipe against the ashtray, his brows furrowed.

"Why are you doing this, Erin?" he asked softly. "What do you gain by taking a pro-SAC stance?"

Her heart hammered and her mouth went dry. "The facts dictate the stance, Bruce."

His mouth curled in irritation. "Come on! You were asked to research this article and take a certain slant on it. It's not as if I haven't given you similar assignments before, that I haven't asked for the same thing."

"In the past the facts happened to support the slant," she replied cooly.

He drew out a tobacco pouch and angrily stuffed his pipe. "Do you know what's at stake here?" he ground out.

"I have a pretty good idea."

"From the start I tried to tell you how damned important this article is, Erin."

Abruptly she got up, unable to sit still for a moment longer. Her skirt swirled around her slender legs as she walked toward the corner opposite where Bruce sat. "I won't write something that isn't substantiated by facts, Bruce, and that's final. The end. Call it what you want. I just won't prostitute myself in that manner."

He rose, shaking his head angrily. "Prostitution. You know, that's an interesting choice of words, Erin," he said softly.

Her nostrils flared with fury. In an instant she realized he was referring to her personal relationship with Ty. "You're overstepping your—"

"Am I?" he barked. He picked up her article and threw it down on his desk with disgust. "He must be one hell of a man to turn *your* head! I never thought you'd fall for such an obvious ploy. You, of all people, Erin."

"Now, just a minute, Bruce!" She half-ran to his desk and faced him squarely. "Are you accusing me of being sexually blackmailed by Captain Phillips?" Her voice quavered with barely contained anger. "Well?"

"I told you what I'd be forced to do if you didn't turn in a suitable article," he returned coldly. "What do you think it will do to your credentials as a reporter when it comes out in print that you swapped your professional integrity for a couple of nights in bed?"

Erin took a step back, deeply shocked. In all the years she had worked for Bruce, he had never come close to being so underhanded. Frozen by amazement, she stood in openmouthed silence.

"And if you print that kind of garbage, you'll have a lawsuit on your hands, Mr. Lansbury," came a deep voice from the door.

Erin gasped and whirled around. "Ty!"

He was dressed in his Air Force uniform, his body tense and shoulders thrown back. His eyes were thundercloud-black and narrowed on Bruce. For a brief instant his gaze swept over Erin; then he returned his attention to her boss and walked into the office as quietly, and confidently as a cat hunting its prey. He halted inches from the desk.

Erin felt suddenly weak. Her thoughts whirled as she stared at Ty. He hadn't expected to return to Sawyer until the twenty-ninth! What had happened? But it didn't matter. He was here, defending her, protecting her.

Bruce glowered at Ty. "Captain Phillips, I presume?" he drawled. Then his voice hardened. "You haven't got a lawsuit. The Air Force isn't going to get embroiled in this messy little tempest in a teapot. We both know that. The military stooping to sue a publishing company? That would make even better press, wouldn't it?"

Ty slowly removed his cap and placed it on the desk in front of him. "I'm not here in an official Air Force capacity, Mr. Lansbury. I'm here strictly as a civilian with certain rights, which seem to be in need of protection." Ty glanced at Erin. "And if you think you're going to drag her down in the filth of your blackmail, you're mistaken," he snarled softly. "You print whatever you want about the Triad. I don't give a damn what you say. But if you so much as intimate anything about the personal, private relationship between Erin and me, I'll hang you." His words were chilling. "You and I both know you have no proof, only conjecture. And that won't stand up in any court of law."

Bruce's face paled. "Do you have any idea of the size of our legal department, Captain?" he said coldly.

"You don't scare me, Lansbury."

Bruce's eyes narrowed speculatively. "No? Then what does?" He looked at Erin. "She's as good as fired right now. Was it worth it, Erin? You're going to throw it all away on this lousy SAC article?"

She trembled, anger momentarily dimming her vision. She had taken several steps forward before she felt Ty's reassuring hand on her arm.

"No," she heard him order quietly. "Let him throw the accusations. It's so much more evidence to be used later, if necessary."

Bruce laughed harshly. "You're a bigger fool than I thought, Captain. If I hadn't seen it with my own eyes, I'd never have believed it! I thought patriotism, high moral standards, and blind honor were dead. I can see I'm wrong." He pursed his lips, watching Ty carefully.

Ty pulled Erin closer, keeping a steadying hand on her arm. "We're from two different worlds, Lansbury," he said coldly. "And don't talk to me about honor. You don't know the meaning of the word." He jabbed his finger at the stunned editor. "Don't let me see anything about our personal lives in print. If you do, you and I will tangle personally. And I'm not in the habit of losing the battles I fight. Do we understand each other?"

The silence lengthened. Erin stared at them, frozen, acutely aware of the vast gulf between them. Bruce was prepared to abandon his principles to keep his job, to maintain his political standing with the publisher. Ty would never forsake his values, no matter what the cost. She would lose her job if she sided with Ty. Suddenly it seemed a small price to pay for what was important in her life. She touched Ty's arm.

"Enough's been said," she told him in a low voice.

She lifted her head, meeting her boss's gaze. "Under the circumstances, Bruce, I find it impossible to stay. I know you'll accept my resignation."

Ty's eyes on her were filled with pride. Then he glared at the editor. "Are we clear?" he demanded, his voice as sharp as a blade.

Bruce nodded imperceptibly. "Clear," he agreed.

Ty gently urged Erin toward the door. "Let's go."

Numbly Erin did as he asked, barely aware of the employees who had gathered at the end of the hall. She walked into her own office, at a loss for words. Ty shut the door quietly behind them.

"I'm sorry," he said, coming over to her. "Get your purse and coat and we'll go."

She gave him a stricken look, standing inches from him. "Go where?"

He reached out, the harsh lines of his mouth softening, the anger fading from his eyes as he gazed down at her. "Home," he whispered. "Back to Michigan. With me."

Erin was stunned by the turn of events and grateful for Ty's supporting arm around her waist as they returned to her apartment, where she packed enough clothes for several days. The shock of seeing him and quitting her job had left her reeling. Saying little, he simply kept her close to his side.

When they were on the way to the airport, the questions finally came together in Erin's mind. "I thought you weren't off duty until the twenty-ninth," she said, catching his gaze.

He gave her a swift embrace. "We got finished early." He grinned broadly, the lines of tension in his face finally easing. "Call it pure Irish luck, honey. I wanted to surprise you."

"You surprised me, all right," she muttered. "How long were you standing outside Bruce's door?"

His mouth thinned. "Long enough to hear all his accusations. Your secretary told me you were in his office. I could hear the two of you going at it clear down the hall. So did half the people in the office."

Erin buried her face in her hands. "Oh, Lord, I should have remembered to shut his door."

Ty chuckled and pulled her head against his shoulder. "You know something?" he whispered. "You'd make a hell of an SAC crew member. Standing there taking the heat and not backing down one inch from what you believed." His eyes shone with admiration for her. "I'm proud of you."

"But you and everyone I met at the base have that kind of commitment."

An indulgent smile curved his mouth. "Maybe you've been living in the wrong world, darlin'."

Her heart flowered, and she trembled at the suggestion in his softly spoken words. She buried her head against him. "I've been so miserable without you, Ty."

"No," he countered gently, "We've *both* been miserable without each other. But that's going to change soon. Very soon."

Once they were aboard the commercial jet, Erin leaned back in her seat and closed her eyes, feeling incredibly weary. Ty picked up her hand and cradled it in his. "All right?" he asked, concerned.

She managed a weak smile. "I'm fine," she whispered.

"You're tired. Try and sleep," he urged.

He was right; the need to sleep was almost overpowering. She was safe, he was here, and that was all that mattered. She murmured something inaudible and rested her head against his broad shoulder, allowing sleep to steal over her.

It was dark when Ty pulled the black TransAm into the garage. Erin had awakened when they'd landed at Marquette Airport, amazed to see the large accumulation of snow. It slowly dawned on her that they were only miles from the Canadian border. She remained in a cocoon of relaxation and Ty seemed to realize that she didn't want to talk, only to touch him, as he led her from the car into the warm, quiet house.

"Come on, sleepyhead, you're due for some downtime."

Erin followed him down the carpeted hall to the first bedroom on the right. He opened her suitcase and pulled out a silk nightgown, which he laid on the bed. "Get undressed and into bed," he ordered.

She looked at the nightgown. "But—"

He gripped her arms and brought her against him, kissing her parted lips. "No arguments, my banshee witch. Not tonight. It's been a very long, hard day for both of us. We need a good night's sleep, honey. Just do as I ask. I'll be back in a few minutes. I have to check in with the squadron by phone."

Snuggling down between the cool crisp sheets, Erin dozed. Somewhere in her dazed mind, her heart whispered that she was finally home, truly home for the first time in her life. She allowed the fingers of sleep to steal her away.

During the night she awoke briefly, her head resting against Ty's shoulder, her arm and leg thrown casually across his warm hard body. A sensation of utter joy enveloped her as she nuzzled his jaw like a lost kitten, immediately aware of his arm tightening in answer against her shoulder. Sighing softly, she gave in to an enveloping blanket of healing sleep.

Erin awoke to the scolding of blue jays outside the bedroom window. Next to her, Ty groaned and muttered an oath. A smile curved her mouth as she stretched languidly at his side, running her fingers across his naked chest. Delighting in the play of the hard muscles, she became aware of his pounding heart beating against her ear. The jays squawked raucously.

"Damn them," Ty growled, rolling from his back to his side, pinning Erin beneath him.

She smiled into his sleepy face. His dark hair was tousled, his features boyishly vulnerable, his blue eyes devouring her in the silence. She stifled a laugh, listening as the birds flew from one corner of the house to the other. "That's some alarm clock," she noted, reaching up and smoothing the rebellious hair off Ty's forehead.

He captured her hand and pinned it against the pillow near her head. He claimed her lips, parting them, his tongue caressing the corners of her mouth. She moaned and guilelessly arched her body upward, meeting the hard planes of his. He pulled away, studying her in the gray dawn light, his eyes moving hungrily over her features. "God, you're lovely when you wake up," he murmured. He released her wrist and slid his fingers through her dark hair, his expression wistful. "Do you know how many times I've dreamed of waking up in this house with you here in my arms?"

She barely shook her head, mesmerized by the incredible warmth in his eyes, and the rough growl in his voice. Thoughtfully he stroked her temple, pushing the featherlike tendrils of hair behind her ear. She quivered at his touch. His fingers were like a brush kissing the canvas of a painting. Her lashes, long and thick, fell against her cheeks. "I never thought I'd be here again," she choked out softly.

Ty raised himself on one elbow, lingering above her, his hand resting against the slender curve of her neck and shoulder. "Why?" he asked, his thumb idly outlining her jaw.

She met his concerned gaze. A lump was beginning to form in her throat. "I . . . just never thought . . ." She gave a helpless shrug. "Meeting you was a dream come true, Ty," she began haltingly. "I was realistic about our situation. We lived so far apart. Our life-styles were— well . . ."

He shook his head, taking her into his arms, holding her tightly. "I know," he soothed, burying his face in her hair. He pressed her against the bed and cupped her face. "I think we've taken those hurdles pretty well, don't you?"

She nodded. "One hurdle is definitely out of the way," she murmured. "My job."

He scowled. "Do you regret quitting, Erin?"

"No, not really." She caressed his shoulder, her fingers trailing down his arm to his hand, which rested against her hip. "I've known Bruce for a long time," she said, "and I've seen him put incredible pressure on other reporters. But he never did it to me."

"He probably knew you'd buck the issues," Ty growled.

She frowned. "I don't know. I can't figure out why he'd try to force me to write something I didn't believe."

Ty pursed his lips. "I think there's a pretty simple explanation, honey. He thought he could use your hatred of the Air Force to get you to criticize SAC. He's not a stupid man. The only problem was," he added, regarding her thoughtfully, "you were intelligent enough to make up your own mind."

"Then he's even more despicable than I thought," she answered angrily. "That's horrible, Ty!"

He grinned. "Easy, my banshee witch, you're starting to show that volatile temper of yours."

She struggled into a sitting position, distraught by thoughts of Bruce's manipulation of her. "I just can't believe it!" she breathed angrily. "He deliberately chose *me* for the assignment, hoping to use my personal grief and anger to slant the story!" She clenched her fists convulsively in front of her knees. "I was so stupid not to realize it before."

Ty pulled her back into his arms. "Come here," he ordered huskily. He simply held her, caressing her back and shoulders, murmuring calm words.

Meanwhile the world was waking up around them. The slanting rays of the sun were beginning to poke through the window. The steady beat of Ty's heart next to Erin's ear helped her to forget her anger. Finally she said, "You knew all along, didn't you?"

He took a deep breath and exhaled slowly. "Yes," he whispered.

"If you saw what he was doing, why didn't you tell me?"

He leaned down, kissing her cheek. "Would you have believed me, darlin'? Ty Phillips, the Air Force captain who works for SAC?"

She closed her eyes, forced to admit she wouldn't have believed him. She caressed his shoulder gently. "So you just waited for the inevitable confrontation and arrived just in time to pick up the pieces."

"One thing you should know about bomber pilots, honey. We learn to be patient. But it wasn't easy. I had to convince you that my intentions were honorable, and genuine. When you told me about your husband's death, I put two and two together real fast. I knew at once what Bruce Lansbury was doing, and it took everything I had to keep my mouth shut. I was in no position to make you aware of how he was using you. All I could do was pray you'd see the truth without me losing you."

Ty eased her back on the bed, a wry smile on his strong mouth. "Another thing about bomber pilots you're going to find out," he muttered softly, nibbling her ear, sending delicious tingles throughout her body, "is that we're tenacious. Once we find someting we like, we just don't let go. Not without a hell of a fight."

Erin sighed langourously, responding to his arousing touch. "Never let me go," she whispered breathlessly against his descending mouth. "Never..."

This time his kiss was possessive and demanding. Gone was the gentleness. Instead there was raw desire that he had held in check until this moment. His mouth stole her breath away. He held her heart and soul captive within his masculine embrace. His tongue moved deliciously inside her mouth, igniting fires deep within her body. She moaned, wanting, needing him fully, aware of his fingers expertly stripping off her white silk nightgown. Her skin prickled pleasurably as he slowly pulled the material away, exposing her full, taut breasts.

He caressed them ardently, teasing the nipples until they rose to his touch. He dragged his mouth from her throbbing lips and trailed kisses across her neck and shoulders, finally moving to the hardened peaks. Her fingers gripped his shoulders and a soft cry was torn from her lips. The urge to be one with him became overwhelming. She shuddered in sweet anticipation as he slid his hand across her flat stomach, parting her thighs.

Her breath came in shallow gasps as he shifted above her. He whispered her name lovingly, his hand beneath her hips, guiding her upward, meeting her, melding in fiery union before his mouth descended on hers. She was freed from the earth, soaring ever higher on wings of passion that held her in sweet torture. Each branding touch against her body, each whispered word against her mouth, acted on her like magic as Ty coaxed her to shamelessly savor their love. Suddenly a burst of fire exploded within her, and she tensed against him, crying out in joy. He held her so tightly that the breath seemed robbed from her body, but she was light-headed with euphoria. Moments later she felt his own release and smiled because he had found fulfillment in her.

A tremulous smile played on her lips as he rolled over, bringing her to rest on top of him. She lay against him, her hair spilling across his chest. Their hearts thundered in unison, and she kissed his neck and jaw, tasting the saltiness, reveling in the pleasure she had shared with him.

He caressed her possessively. "You have a beautiful back," he murmured. His moving fingers sent shivers flowing across her sensitive skin. "Smooth. A nice deep indentation..." He shared a tender smile with her. "You're beautiful all over, darlin'. Incredibly loving and beautiful." He placed kisses on her eyes, nose, and finally her lips.

"How can you make me so happy?" She sighed languorously.

"Because I love you, that's why."

Her heart leaped and she lost herself within his warming blue eyes. "And I love you," she said solemnly.

"We've loved each other since the day we met, honey. But at first neither one of us could admit it."

Erin closed her eyes, recalling the pain of being apart from him for months. "Is there anything you don't know?" she asked. "I didn't realize I was falling in love with you until that horrible experience in the hyperbaric chamber." She shivered, remembering. "Just your touch, Ty . . . your voice." She met his curiously bright gaze. "I gave myself over to you, something I hadn't done since Steve died. I thought I always had to be strong and self-reliant. I'd just never met a man I felt I could collapse against and trust to take care of me. Not until you came along."

He captured her lips in a kiss filled with tenderness. "You need taking care of, my banshee witch," he murmured throatily. "And you're right—you are strong and self-sufficient. I want you that way. But I also love the soft, feminine side of you."

She rubbed her cheek against his rough one. "Don't worry. You automatically bring that out in me! Around you I have to carry Kleenex."

Ty laughed. "They'll be tears of happiness as well as tears of growing, honey."

She ran her fingers through the dark hair on his chest, thinking. Finally she asked, "Where is all of this leading us, Ty?"

He grinned. "That's why I stole you away for seven days. I want the time to talk, explore, and share with you, Erin Quinlan. We deserve it."

She returned his smile, feeling as if she would explode from happiness. "I think you're right."

12

ON THANKSGIVING DAY it began to snow in mid-afternoon. Large wet flakes fell silently through the slender twigs and branches of the trees that surrounded the house. Inside, Erin turned away from the window and back to the kitchen, where the mouth-watering aroma of a fully roasted turkey filled the room. Ty leaned over her shoulder as she basted the golden-brown bird.

"Well?" he asked.

She turned to him and melted beneath his penetrating gaze. "It's done."

He straightened up and gave her a pat on the rear. "Great!" Taking silverware from the drain board, he began to set the tastefully decorated dining room table. Erin hummed softly as she scooped succulent sage dressing from the bird into a white china bowl.

For Erin the day held a great deal of personal meaning. She and Ty had worked in the kitchen after sharing an early shower. Ty had proudly produced a twenty-pound turkey from the refrigerator, making Erin laugh. They wouldn't make a dent in that turkey! But Ty grinned boyishly and shrugged, saying they'd be eating a lot of turkey sandwiches at lunch for the next seven days.

Erin was busy stirring the gravy when the phone rang. Ty picked it up in the kitchen, watching her as he leaned against the refrigerator.

"Hello? Oh, hi, Barry. What's up?"

Ty's expression immediately changed. Barry was his copilot, or co. She stirred the gravy more slowly, listening to Ty's half of the conversation.

"Yeah . . . yeah . . . She what?" He glanced up at Erin, grinning. "Hold on, I'll ask her." He couldn't suppress a chuckle. "It's my co, Erin. He and his wife, Carolyn, invited the rest of our crew over for Thanksgiving dinner, but they burned the turkey!"

"Oh, no! They must feel terrible!"

Ty kept his hand over the receiver. "Look, the guys knew you were coming up here for a week. Usually we share holidays together if we can. Carol and Barry were kind enough to take on the whole crew plus their families this time around. Usually we hold the parties here because I live off base and the house can hold a lot of people."

Erin smiled, anticipating what he was going to ask. "Why not ask them to come here and share our turkey?" she suggested. "Lord knows, we've got enough for an army!"

Ty winced. "Air Force, please. Not the doggy Army. Have some sensitivity," he teased, his grin widening.

Erin laughed. "Okay."

He searched her face, as if to make sure she didn't mind the unexpected guests. "Look, they all know this is a special time for you and me," he began huskily. "I don't want you to feel obligated just because—"

She shook her head. "Ty Phillips, you tell them to get over here. I won't take no for an answer."

He winked at her. "That's my gal." He removed his

hand from the mouthpiece. "Hey, Barry, bring the crew over. We've got enough for everybody." He continued to smile at her, his eyes warm with affection. "Yes, bring the kids, too. The dogs?" He lifted an eyebrow. Erin nodded. "Yeah, why not? We can let them run in the fenced-in area out back. A little snow won't hurt those ugly mutts. Okay, see you in about half an hour. Bye."

Erin had returned to the gravy when she felt Ty walk up behind her. His arms went around her waist and he pulled her back against him, resting his head on her shoulder. "You're a special lady," he whispered.

Snow was falling heavily by the time four cars pulled into the driveway. Erin had rearranged the table setting, while Ty had set up a card table and TV trays in the basement game room for the children. Smiling at him, Erin felt prepared to handle the boisterous crew coming up the walk.

Ty dragged her from the kitchen, the apron still around her waist and the potato masher in her hand, as they piled into the foyer. Children ranging in age from a few months to early teens smiled politely at Erin. Ty pulled her close to him as he began introducing everyone. The wives responded enthusiastically and greeted her without reserve.

Carol grimaced. "Erin, we brought over the rest of the dinner—yams, salads, vegetables, and desserts. Can you use them?"

"With this crowd?" She laughed. "Sure. Come on, you can help me set up a command post in the kitchen, and we'll get everyone settled down for dinner."

"Hey," John called, grinning mischievously at Ty, "she's already sounding like an AC's wife. Taking charge just comes with the territory, huh, Erin?"

She blushed as they all laughed, but, despite her embarrassment, she felt like an accepted member of the group. "I—well, I didn't mean for it to sound—"

"John, leave her alone," Ray, the nav, interrupted. "Can't you see you're embarrassing her?" He then promptly turned beet-red himself when everyone glanced over at him.

"Damn mushrooms." Guns chortled. "Come on, men, let's head for the basement, where we can watch the football game in peace. I've got some heavy bets running with the other gunners."

As the children and men trooped downstairs, Erin was grateful that Ty stayed. He and the women took over the kitchen. As they went about final preparations for the meal, the squeals and laughter of the children, along with the collective groans and cheers from the men, floated up the stairs.

The house rang with warmth and camaraderie all afternoon. Much later, after they'd all eaten a delicious meal and not much remained of the twenty-pound turkey, Ty exchanged a silent, meaningful glance with Erin as she rested on the couch, balancing a plate of pumpkin pie on her lap. Adults and children were sprawled out all over the living room like contented puppies. The teenagers had gone outside to have a snowball fight.

"Hey, Erin," Ray called from his position on the floor, "Did Ty tell you how much he pined away for you while we were stuck on that mission? He must have lost ten pounds from not eating right."

She glanced at Ty, who sat at her left. "No, he didn't tell me," she said in a mock-accusing tone.

"Yeah," Barry chimed in, "you should have seen him, Erin. Talk about a long face!"

"And a real moody bastard," Ray added. "Man, he was a bear with a capital *B*."

"That bad, huh?" she teased Ty.

He returned her smile. "It was pretty bad. These poor slobs had to put up with my natural Irish moodiness."

"You should have seen his face when we were relieved from the mission early," Ray added. "I've never seen anybody pack as fast as he did!"

Ty slid his hand beneath Erin's, holding it firmly. "And I suppose you weren't glad to be coming home to see Cherie?" he asked. "You didn't act exactly gloomy, turkey."

Guns grinned. "He's a mushroom, remember? Of course, they are a couple of birds down in that hole, come to think of it."

"Stuff it, Guns," Ray responded politely, making everyone laugh.

"So all of you have the next six days off?" Erin asked the crew.

"Yes, ma'am," Guns answered, giving his wife a leering glance.

"Is this the time you catch up on all the projects the women couldn't or didn't want to do?" she continued.

Barry grinned. "You mean like getting cars fixed and patching the roof?"

"Yes."

Carol gave her husband a warning look. "Don't let him fool you, Erin. We do everything. Things *always* break down while the men are away. We learned a long time ago to either fix it ourselves or call someone who can."

The EWO, Skip Helman, grinned knowingly. "Yeah, so by the time we get back, there's plenty of time for other, more important things." He gave his brunette wife a quick hug.

"Oh," Erin countered lamely.

John laughed heartily. "Did you notice the number of kids running around? The stork sure didn't bring them."

"Yeah, we really work hard when we get home," Guns boasted. His wife gave him a jab in the ribs and he feigned injury.

"Ease off," Ty warned them, trying to be serious. "Erin can't take you guys all at once."

Ray rolled over on his back and tucked his hands under his balding head. "Ah, she'll get used to it, Ty. We're such a lovable bunch."

Late that night Erin rested her head against Ty's leg, idly watching the flames in the fireplace licking upward in the chimney while she drank apricot brandy. It was nearly midnight, and silence had stolen over the house. He caressed her hair, his hand lingering on her shoulder. "Quite a day, huh?"

She closed her eyes, warming to his touch. "Mmm, but wonderful. I've never had such a fantastic Thanksgiving. I don't know when I've ever laughed so hard and for so long—especially when Ray tried to bob for that apple and Skip pushed his head under the water. That really wasn't fair." She laughed, picturing the episode. Ty ran his fingers through her hair and pushed himself away from the couch, leaning over where she sat on the floor.

"You're a good sport, you know that?"

She smiled coyly. "Why?"

"Because you made a fool out of yourself like everyone else trying to get an apple. That takes courage in front of a bunch of strangers."

She touched his cheek. Ty captured her hand, and

kissed her palm with tantalizing slowness. "I didn't feel like a stranger," she admitted. "Isn't that funny? Back in New York I doubt I'd have felt as welcome. But here . . ."

Ty released her hand and slid down beside her on the carpet. He poured more apricot brandy into the snifter she cradled in her hands. "Here it's different, honey. SAC forces us to work hard and long, sometimes too much so. But when we get a break, we play hard too. As a crew."

"At everything?" she teased.

"Not quite everything," he answered. He took her into his arms, his mouth descending lightly against her lips, teasing them with his tongue. His breath was moist against her face as she leaned eagerly against his body, hungry for the closeness he offered. Pulling away, he whispered, "Come on. Let's go to bed. It's been a long day and we're both tired."

Six days later, Erin gingerly tested the snow, which was almost knee-deep. She had bundled up in a hip-length lavender ski coat, white knit cap, and mittens, and was waiting patiently for Ty. Her breath formed white clouds in the early afternoon air. The sky was a deep blue, and the sun glinted fiercely off the snow. In the distance, she heard the thunderous growl of B-52's winding up for takeoff.

Some of her ebullient mood faded as she thought of the last week. It had gone by so fast. When had she enjoyed life so fully as with Ty? She rubbed her mittened hands together and moved in a small circle to keep warm. Their time was almost over, and she frowned, unsure of the direction her future would take. She placed her hand over her heart, fiercely aware of the love she felt for Ty. In the past week, he had shared more about his life with her. Their long talks had revealed new aspects of his character, but above all she had come to see just how dedicated he was to his career. She had never realized that men like Ty and his crew existed, and her admiration for them and their families deepened.

At last Ty appeared at the back door and skipped down the wooden steps, a picnic basket in one hand, a blanket in the other. He tossed her a warming smile as he handed her the blanket and promptly slid his arms around her shoulders, drawing her near.

"Almost forgot the mulled wine," he said by way of apology.

"Can't do that," she answered, pretending to be horrified. His blue eyes danced. His ability to express his feelings openly had helped her tremendously to voice her own emotions. He was an inspiration to her in every way.

"I don't think we'll have any problem keeping it hot," he said dryly. "We'll drink it fast once we reach the meadow."

She laughed with him, and they continued to trek toward the same meadow where they had held another picnic weeks ago. After the exhausting walk, Erin was happy to plop down on the blanket. She had never gone on a winter picnic and was thrilled with the idea. As Ty explained, living at a Northern Tier base forced him to be more creative in thinking up ways to spend his leisure hours.

Erin sat expectantly across from him, hands in her

lap, as she watched him open the thermos.

"This is a very special picnic, darlin'," he said, pouring hot, spicy wine into a ceramic mug. Their fingers touched as he handed it to her, and pleasure tingled up her arm. "Careful, you could burn your tongue," he warned.

She held the mug to her lips, inhaling the fruity fragrance. "Mmm, it smells like heaven!"

"No way, gal. *You* smell like heaven. Matter of fact, you *are* heaven." He recapped the thermos and raised his mug, his eyes steady on hers. "Here, I want to make a toast," he said.

Erin caught the husky inflection in his tone. A new expression of seriousness came to his face as he met her widened eyes. "Go ahead," she urged softly, touching his mug with hers.

"Here's to a lifetime of sharing love," he said, watching her closely.

Her lips parted and she stared at him in silence.

"Well?" he prodded gently. "Are you going to drink to that, my lovely banshee witch?"

The pulse leaped at the base of her throat. "You mean—" she stammered.

A lazy smile curved his mouth. "You realize, of course, that if you go back to New York, I'll die of wretched loneliness without you."

She lowered the mug, unable to meet his warming gaze any longer. "Oh, Ty." The moments of silence lengthened between them. She fingered the mug, staring down into the ruby liquid.

"What's going on in your head?" he demanded quietly. "Are you worried about being up here in the middle of nowhere without a job, with no career?"

Erin lifted her chin, eyes filled with tears. "I can free-lance . . ."

Ty tilted his head, studying her. "What then, honey?"

She made a small helpless gesture. "I—I thought all you wanted was an affair. A long-term one, but—"

He reached out and gripped her hand firmly. "I don't go around saying 'I love you' to every woman I meet, Erin. I do love you, and that means one-hundred-percent commitment. Whatever gave you the crazy idea that all I wanted was an affair?"

She sniffed, brushing away a tear. "I never thought we stood a chance, Ty. I live in New York. I have—had—a job there. From the way you talked about your first marriage, I knew you had chosen between a personal commitment and your career. But I can't help feeling that your marriage ended because of more than just your career." She studied him keenly. "You made Anne out to be the victim, but somehow"—she groped for the right words—"somehow I think she contributed to the problems too. It takes two to make a divorce, Ty, not just one. Knowing you as I do, I think you're taking most of the blame on yourself. Is that true?"

He put his mug down and then took hers from her fingers and pulled her into his arms. "You're right on all counts," he said heavily. "Anne had a streak of restlessness I couldn't satisfy, Erin. She craved a more exciting life, a faster pace of living, I suppose." He shrugged helplessly. "What can I say? We were like a plow horse and a thoroughbred in the same hitch. We worked against each other instead of together." He touched her wet cheek, drying it gently. "Part of it was my fault. I was fulfilling some pretty tough career demands at the time. The other was just mismatched personalities. It happens, you know, to more people than I care to think about. I got married too young, when I was too eager about establishing my career."

Erin remained silent for a long time. "What if I have to fly all over the U.S. or Canada to get stories for different magazines and newspapers? Would you object?"

Ty chuckled, nuzzling her ear. "How could I? I'll be flying halfway around the world, taking off on secret missions or just going on long training flights. I'll be gone twenty days out of every month. No, honey, I wouldn't mind. I'd hope that those other ten days we might be together instead of apart."

Erin closed her eyes and sighed. "We'll make the most of those ten days," she promised huskily.

He turned her so that she was resting her back against his bent leg. "Well, will you marry me now?"

She threw her arms around his neck. "Yes!" she whispered fiercely into his ear, "I will!"

He murmured her name, his mouth seeking and finding her lips. She responded passionately to his breath-stealing kiss, content to remain imprisoned within his arms.

His blue eyes danced with a roguish glint as he drew away. He shifted her next to him and dug in his side pocket. "Here," he said, drawing out a velvet gray box, "open this."

He placed it in her waiting hands. She smiled at him as she carefully lifted the lid. Her eyes widened in appreciation as she stared at a dark-blue oval stone in a platinum setting. "It's lovely," she whispered.

"Not the usual diamond ring," he noted.

"I never liked diamonds," she admitted, carefully pulling the ring from the box. Ty placed it on her left hand.

"This is a rare form of tourmaline that I bought a long time ago when I was down in South America on leave." He held her hand up and the color of the stone changed as light refracted through it. "When I saw this stone, it reminded me of a woman whose eyes changed colors depending on her moods." He smiled tenderly down at her. "You're like that, darlin'—moody, unpredictable, willful, part child, part adult. The tourmaline symbolizes a very small part of the vast range of your emotions, all of which I love experiencing."

She gripped his hand, resting her cheek against it, her heart turning over with love. "It's so beautiful," she whispered, fighting back tears of happiness. "I never expected anything, Ty."

He laughed softly and hugged her fiercely. "Banshee witches only cast spells. They don't look into the future," he murmured, kissing her temple. "Let's face it, we're two very unique people, and we'll have a unique marriage. The engagement ring is a symbol of that, a celebration of our individuality. I can't think of a better way to start a wonderful marriage. Can you?"

She gazed down at the ring, which was the color of the sky in which he would continue to fly. To Erin the ring symbolized a proud breed of men and women who believed deeply in what they were doing and were willing to pay the price.

She loved Ty Phillips. His standards and commitment were no higher than her own.

She placed her hands on either side of his face and looked deeply into his eyes. "I've been waiting a lifetime to meet you, darling. This ring is living proof of our love for one another."

He kissed her hands. "What took you so long to come into my life?" he whispered, crushing her in his arms.

She nuzzled beneath his chin, thoroughly content. "I guess good things are just worth waiting for."

"And honey, *you* were worth waiting for, believe me," he said fiercely, covering her lips in a soul-searing kiss.

_____ 06692-3 **THE WAYWARD WIDOW** #81 Anne Mayfield
_____ 06693-1 **TARNISHED RAINBOW** #82 Jocelyn Day
_____ 06694-X **STARLIT SEDUCTION** #83 Anne Reed
_____ 06695-8 **LOVER IN BLUE** #84 Aimée Duvall
_____ 06696-6 **THE FAMILIAR TOUCH** #85 Lynn Lawrence
_____ 06697-4 **TWILIGHT EMBRACE** #86 Jennifer Rose
_____ 06698-2 **QUEEN OF HEARTS** #87 Lucia Curzon
_____ 06850-0 **PASSION'S SONG** #88 Johanna Phillips
_____ 06851-9 **A MAN'S PERSUASION** #89 Katherine Granger
_____ 06852-7 **FORBIDDEN RAPTURE** #90 Kate Nevins
_____ 06853-5 **THIS WILD HEART** #91 Margarett McKean
_____ 06854-3 **SPLENDID SAVAGE** #92 Zandra Colt
_____ 06855-1 **THE EARL'S FANCY** #93 Charlotte Hines
_____ 06858-6 **BREATHLESS DAWN** #94 Susanna Collins
_____ 06859-4 **SWEET SURRENDER** #95 Diana Mars
_____ 06860-8 **GUARDED MOMENTS** #96 Lynn Fairfax
_____ 06861-6 **ECSTASY RECLAIMED** #97 Brandy LaRue
_____ 06862-4 **THE WIND'S EMBRACE** #98 Melinda Harris
_____ 06863-2 **THE FORGOTTEN BRIDE** #99 Lillian Marsh
_____ 06864-0 **A PROMISE TO CHERISH** #100 LaVyrle Spencer
_____ 06865-9 **GENTLE AWAKENING** #101 Marianne Cole
_____ 06866-7 **BELOVED STRANGER** #102 Michelle Roland
_____ 06867-5 **ENTHRALLED** #103 Ann Cristy
_____ 06869-1 **DEFIANT MISTRESS** #105 Anne Devon
_____ 06870-5 **RELENTLESS DESIRE** #106 Sandra Brown
_____ 06871-3 **SCENES FROM THE HEART** #107 Marie Charles
_____ 06872-1 **SPRING FEVER** #108 Simone Hadary
_____ 06873-X **IN THE ARMS OF A STRANGER** #109 Deborah Joyce
_____ 06874-8 **TAKEN BY STORM** #110 Kay Robbins
_____ 06899-3 **THE ARDENT PROTECTOR** #111 Amanda Kent
_____ 07200-1 **A LASTING TREASURE** #112 Cally Hughes $1.95

All of the above titles are $1.75 per copy except where noted

_____ 07201-X **RESTLESS TIDES** #113 Kelly Adams $1.95
_____ 07203-6 **COME WINTER'S END** #115 Claire Evans $1.95
_____ 07204-4 **LET PASSION SOAR** #116 Sherry Carr $1.95
_____ 07205-2 **LONDON FROLIC** #117 Josephine Janes $1.95
_____ 07206-0 **IMPRISONED HEART** #118 Jasmine Craig $1.95
_____ 07207-9 **THE MAN FROM TENNESSEE** #119 Jeanne Grant $1.95
_____ 07208-7 **LAUGH WITH ME, LOVE WITH ME** #120 Lee Damon $1.95
_____ 07209-5 **PLAY IT BY HEART** #121 Vanessa Valcour $1.95
_____ 07210-9 **SWEET ABANDON** #122 Diana Mars $1.95
_____ 07211-7 **THE DASHING GUARDIAN** #123 Lucia Curzon $1.95
_____ 07212-5 **SONG FOR A LIFETIME** #124 Mary Haskell $1.95
_____ 07213-3 **HIDDEN DREAMS** #125 Johanna Phillips $1.95
_____ 07214-1 **LONGING UNVEILED** #126 Meredith Kingston $1.95
_____ 07215-X **JADE TIDE** #127 Jena Hunt $1.95
_____ 07216-8 **THE MARRYING KIND** #128 Jocelyn Day $1.95
_____ 07217-6 **CONQUERING EMBRACE** #129 Ariel Tierney $1.95
_____ 07218-4 **ELUSIVE DAWN** #130 Kay Robbins $1.95
_____ 07219-2 **ON WINGS OF PASSION** #131 Beth Brookes $1.95
_____ 07220-6 **WITH NO REGRETS** #132 Nuria Wood $1.95
_____ 07221-4 **CHERISHED MOMENTS** #133 Sarah Ashley $1.95
_____ 07222-2 **PARISIAN NIGHTS** #134 Susanna Collins $1.95
_____ 07233-0 **GOLDEN ILLUSIONS** #135 Sarah Crewe $1.95